Spytrap

Smoke from his chain-smoked Marlboros fogged the car window. With the tip of my necktie I rubbed clear a circular spot in the condensation. I wanted to watch a team of men in a black Citroen parked facing the U.S. Embassy. This was my opposition.

Thus our spy makes his first move. The condensation is caused by 'the cold rain that makes such a joke of the Vienna summer'.

This little ploy turns out a success, but it is only the prelude to a far more ambitious onslaught against the massed ranks of opposing espionage agencies. And here our very own agent soon discovers he has enemies within his own ranks in addition to the official opposition.

Then he meets a girl 'with oval Mediterranean brown eyes that spoke of olive oil and southern sea and cypresses'. Even a married spy may be overwhelmed by such temptation.

For underneath its veneer of some rather novel (and even comical) espionage this is a love story, a man's love for two women. Although it embraces mad and secret deals in petroleum products, very improbable games of Rugby Union in deepest Czechoslovakia, financial frauds, plots, betrayals, threats and escapes, it is love that is the force that drives – mostly towards disaster.

This original, charming and humorous first novel may loosely be termed 'spoof espionage', but the credibility, pace and romance sweep the reader along towards a trap that few will see coming.

For Anita Elizabeth

SPYTRAP

William Crisp

Macmillan London

ISBN 0 333 33631 3

First published 1982 by
MACMILLAN LONDON LIMITED
London and Basingstoke
Associated companies in Auckland Dallas Delhi Dublin
Hong Kong Johannesburg Lagos Manzini Melbourne Nairobi
New York Singapore Tokyo Washington and Zaria

Typeset in Great Britain by
WESTERN PRINTING SERVICES LTD
Avonmouth, Bristol

Printed in Great Britain by
THE ANCHOR PRESS LIMITED
Tiptree Essex

Bound in Great Britain by
WM. BRENDON AND SON LIMITED
Tiptree Essex

Chapter 1

Rain had begun to fall again, the cold rain that makes such a joke of the Vienna summer.

It was a typical strawberries-and-cream, sunny lawns and tennis summer in England. Most regions of the United States had already wilted in semi-tropical humidity. But Vienna was shrouded in chill as the rain dripped from the chestnut trees facing the American embassy on Boltzmanngasse.

'Their communications are coming through good on our radio intercept,' my driver told me.

Smoke from his chain-smoked Marlboros fogged the car window. With the tip of my necktie I rubbed clear a circular spot in the condensation. I wanted to watch a team of men in a black Citroen parked facing the US embassy. This was my opposition. They wanted to pull a snatch job on our embassy code technician – and they had no business putting their paws on him.

'Turn up the volume,' I told the driver.

We listened as the men in the black Citroen engaged in all sorts of cypher words with their communications van. Their verbosity was juvenile.

My driver ground out his cigarette in the ashtray 'They blabber too much.'

'That is because they assume their scrambling device is completely secure.'

'Our security communications equipment is two generations ahead of anything they manufacture.'

'They make good colour TV sets,' I snapped.

We were both tense. This was a tricky assignment.

My embassy's security chief was very worried. If the opposition grabbed our code man they would steam him like a Maine lobster. Steam him here in Vienna in their embassy, thumbing their nose at the bumbling, supposedly neutral Austrians.

'Ever see that man in the Citroen?' my driver asked.

'He's highly trained. Nasty brute. He goes in for Kung Fu, judo, hand chops.'

'That's ridiculous.'

'Once when I was in Moscow he was tailing somebody. I was having a drink in the dollar bar and in he came and I looked at the edge of his hand.'

'Calloused.'

'From chopping bricks in half. Smashing lumber.'

'Won't they ever realise? You can't go around doing that sort of stuff.'

'He thinks the Cold War is still on.'

'They all do. That way they can demand more money.'

'It's totally childish. At least we are beginning to show some refinement.'

With the cigarette smoke and wet air, sitting in the car had become increasingly unpleasant. My necktie pinched my throat. I ripped the collar open. My suit felt wrinkled and baggy. I wanted to get out of there and drive home and take a shower. Clean up. Wash away the stale sweat and tension. I closed my eyes, breathed very slowly, and fought against the almost uncontrollable urge to abandon the operation. During an assignment you can never allow yourself to think about creature comforts. That is because in this profession a great deal of working time consists of boredom, late night waiting in parked cars, rain, chill, sweaty collars or unbearable heat. You can never let yourself start thinking about taking a shower. Or sipping a neat dram of Scotch whisky. Tonight that would be really outstanding. Naturally the puritans in my administrative section strictly prohibited boozing and Scotch and Bourbon on an active assignment.

My driver nodded at the scrambler-intercept device.

'There they go blaring away again. They sound worried.'

Essentially, the opposition leader was telling his communications van that the target – our embassy code man – was now so delayed that it was dangerous for them to stick around. There was a lot of jabber to and fro and several crude expressions. I translated some of this for my driver.

'They are pushy, nasty bastards.'

'Yes. They think they can operate with impunity in Vienna,' I replied, sucking wet air through the side window vent. 'They have never outlived their conquering Occupation mentality. As far as they are concerned the Austrian police are terrified to lay a finger on them—'

'Look,' he hissed, 'he's coming!'

I wiped the windshield clean. Very slowly, like a man treading on the edge of eternal perdition, our code clerk walked toward the Citroen.

Their scrambler squawked with triumph. I listened to the karate-chopping chief brief his team. He of course told me exactly what moves to expect.

Then and there our code clerk had one final attack of jitters. He hesitated. Stopped, fumbled for a cigarette. Looked at the Citroen, then turned back in the direction of the American embassy building.

Karate-man was a little rattled. More scrambled radio communications.

'Cold feet,' commented my driver. He had been on a lot of these operations. He knew the signs, like

Hawkeye or Deerslayer trailing Virginia deer in a Fenimore Cooper novel.

'They always get cold feet before they sell out. He'll turn around.'

I hoped to hell he would do it quick. Then we could barge in and break up this ridiculous scenario. Maybe I could get home for a late supper. If my wife stayed up to cook it. She didn't like these late-night Viennese assignments any better than I did.

What would she cook? Ham and eggs. That would be wonderful coming in out of the rain. Fresh farmers' eggs bought at the open-air market.

'You're right,' whispered my driver, 'here he comes back.'

The disgraceful code clerk turned around, smoked his cigarette down to the stub, and shuffled back in the direction of the enemy Citroen.

'We should go now, chief?' my driver asked anxiously.

'Wait one.'

It was then that I fired off a radio message to our embassy control room. I waited for the acknowledgement that they had complied with my directive, then opened the car door.

'OK, move in on them.'

Here we go again. Once more into the breach. It never gets any easier. I suppose I'm young for this game. That was why my driver was so much older and experienced. If I blew the assignment or got shaky he would pick up the pieces.

But I wasn't going to get shaky.

I strode down the centre of the street towards the Citroen. The opposition team swung open the car doors just as I reached the rear fender. Obviously they had spotted us. But we had split their attention. They still intended to jerk the code man from the sidewalk and throw him into the back seat.

'Hey you!' the enemy team leader yelled in my direction. 'Get out of the street!'

Without replying I performed the simple act of extracting a Bic ballpoint pen from my jacket pocket, bent over and jammed the pen point into the air valve on the expensive Michelin rear tyre.

ZZZZZZZZZZZZZZZZZSSSSSSSSSSSSSSSSSSss sssss s s.

The tyre went as flat as a bad joke.

Two things happened. Their driver yanked out some sort of fancy .38 calibre automatic pistol and pointed it at my midsection. Second, their razzle-dazzle operation leader released the code clerk and rushed around the Citroen toward me. I simply stepped around in the opposite direction and wound up beside our code man before their leader could scramble back and aim a karate chop at my thorax.

'One moment please,' I told him.

He curled catlike on the balls of his feet but held back his punch.

'This chap,' I nodded at my petrified code clerk, 'is an employee of my embassy. He is not to enter your automobile. And I would caution you to avoid violence. With your deflated rear tyre, dear sir, you are ill-placed to attempt the proverbial get-away.'

I turned to the would-be defector.

'One presumes you have been pressured to defect because of currency transactions or some other mild offence?'

'Come on you *aparatacek*!' the opposition leader bellowed. 'Get in the car!'

The little man blanched white with fear. Gently I pressed his arm for reassurance.

'I can't say you will not face a reprimand. But if you get in my car I can guarantee that you will not be judicially punished.'

'How can I believe that?' the little man quaked.

'You'll get the knife in the basement!' the opposition leader hissed.

'You'd know, luv,' I shrugged.

'I bear a promise from our ambassador,' I continued in order to soothe the man's nerves. 'In writing. You will be transferred home and retained in the service. Hear me. We all make error. You will be far away from these, these provocateurs. The problem won't rise again.'

Their driver yelled he was going to start shooting. At that instant a white Volkswagen swerved in behind us. The car carried flashing blue lights and the inscription POLIZEI. Cops. They had arrived, of course, since my embassy had telephoned the Vienna police immediately after my radio request.

'*Guten abend, die Herrschaften*,' said the police officer from under his peaked cap as he opened the door of the Volkswagen. 'At your service.'

'*Grüss Gott*,' I answered politely. Obviously my opponent was inarticulate in the German language. He stood there confused, mouth agape, baffled as to why the Vienna police should have arrived at this precise moment. I nodded in his direction and spoke in German. 'This gentleman appears in need of your assistance, as he has a flat tyre.'

'Are you a member of the Austrian Automobile Club?' the cop asked him with knee-jerk instinctive bureaucracy. My nemesis glared in rage, realising my ploy. But with the police officer standing there he was powerless to seize the code clerk. The policeman proceeded to offer solicitous advice on repair shops and mobile service units.

As planned, I profited from all this divertimento to take hold of our embassy clerk and lead him away to our limousine. My enemy was furious but he could not detach himself from the police officer. Having thus neatly extracted ourselves, we drove across the wet city. The red trams rattled along their rails as we jolted over the cobblestones. Lights blazed from the Burgtheater. Gentlemen in tuxedos and ladies in long evening dresses stood under umbrellas waiting for taxis.

'Everything in order?' I asked my driver.

'No tails.'

'The key, as always, is to proceed with legality, method, and moderation,' I sighed with fatigue. 'Thank God we were not so stupid to carry weapons.'

'Completely agree. Keep it simple. No violence.'

'Did you mean that about the written assurance?' timorously queried the little code clerk.

I was too weary to go into further explanations. I reached into my breast pocket and handed him a sealed envelope with the ambassador's personal stationery.

'Keep it as a souvenir.'

By God I was tired. If reason had not prevailed out there in the street that barbarian opposition team could have started blasting away. I tried to relax, breathed slowly, felt my stomach muscles unknot. But my shirt hung in sodden wet creases along my back muscles.

Once we were inside our compound I took the elevator up to the security office and signed the night register. Gorev, the night duty officer, was just putting down the telephone receiver.

'I hear it went very routine.'

'If you call that kind of thing routine.'

'Everyone is relieved. The ambassador has just been notified and he extends congratulations.'

'When do we send the code clerk for reposting to

Moscow?' I asked.

'Aeroflot 102 via Kiev tomorrow at 10:20. I'll have Zavich acting as escort. You go home and get some sleep.'

I took the elevator down and backed my Lada out of our Soviet embassy car park.

The drive across Vienna to my apartment in the 19th District took another twenty minutes, so that made it exactly 1a.m. when I got in. My wife was dozing on the couch in front of the TV set. She was in her bathrobe and had smeared her face with night cream. Manuscript pages from her doctoral thesis had slid off the table and scattered across the carpet. An economics textbook lay open on the desk.

She kissed me sleepily.

'A long evening. They keep you out too late.'

'What's left to eat? Ham and eggs?'

'*Bliny*. They're cold. Should I heat them up?'

'Very well.'

'I'll warm up the *bliny*. And I bought some of that French wine in the commissary this afternoon.'

Coming from the Soviet Union, my wife doesn't know a great deal about wines. Not many of us do. It's the harsh climate.

'Red or white?'

'That red beaujolais.'

'Any Scot whisky?'

'Yes, a new bottle too.'

I wondered what the American karate man was now telling his superiors. At the all-powerful Central Intelligence Agency cover office inside the American embassy. 'Sorry chief, the Russians took back their code clerk'?

'I'll drink Scotch.'

'Come in the kitchen while I cook,' said my wife, Olga.

‘Anatoli has written,’ she said. Anatoli is our thirteen-year-old son who lives with Olga’s parents in Moscow.

‘What does he say about his ice hockey?’

‘The trainer says he skates very well and will begin as a forward,’ said Olga, above the hissing frying pan and the warmed-up, pancake-like *bliny*.

Chapter 2

It should be clarified that my employer is the *Komitet Gosudarspvennoy Bezopasnosti*, or, the Soviet Committee for State Security. This is usually abbreviated in Britain and the United States as the KGB. I am a professional intelligence officer.

'. . . *Tovarishchi, nam pridyotcya chto to delat*', Chervenkov, the Soviet Embassy Labour Attaché, convened our discussion the morning after the abortive defection of our code clerk. 'The first point,' he intoned in his bass voice, 'is to establish why the Americans have initiated this action against us . . .'

We were seated in the security cell on the fifth floor of the Soviet embassy building, number 45, Reisnerstrasse, Vienna III. The security cell is a 20×10 metre plexiglass soundproof compartment anchored on plastic stanchions. Wireless, the chamber is lit by neon lighting from the outer room in which it is housed. Bathed in radio waves from an ultrasonic transmitter, there is no known method for a hostile listener to penetrate discussions inside the compartment.

Seven of us had entered the chamber. The Ambassador: portly, rotund and comfortable in his three-piece suit, who sat in silence and concentrated on arranging ball-point pens in geometric forms ranging from isosceles triangles to unequal hexagons upon the green baize table covering.

On his right sat Chervenkov. Perhaps once in every two weeks Chervenkov might touch on some activity which related to his cover assignment as Labour

Attaché. I recall once or twice he had returned with distaste from attendance at an Austrian trade union conference. But the majority of his working hours were devoted to his position as KGB *Rezident*. Chervenkov was the top-ranking Soviet intelligence official in Austria. He hailed from the Crimea, as was evident from the swarthy trace of Tartar blood in his lineage. Above bushy eyebrows his black hair was brushed straight back over the block of his head. This gave him the profile of a battering ram.

Three other KGB specialists sat at Chervenkov's side, but I concentrated on the man at the far end of the table. This was my enemy Razin.

Throughout many past security meetings I have spent hours doodling and sketching Razin's rat-like skull, pointed teeth and thinning, mouse-brown hair. He suffers from a rare allergy which has inflamed the capillary system throughout his white scalp. Inescapable are his lashless eyelids which protrude over phlegmy grey eyes. Unable to read texts without the aid of black-rimmed spectacles, Razin is too vain to wear glasses at meetings where the Ambassador or Chervenkov are present.

Razin has spent his lifetime in the KGB's counter-intelligence branch and is chief of embassy security. Assignment to the Vienna post had come only after a career of toil in the Moscow bureaucracy, assignments to Kiev, Kharkov and the deep provinces of Asiatic Russia. I suppose his hatred of me stemmed from the ease – at a relatively young age – with which I had received my first assignments abroad to London and Washington. Razin lived with one obsession: that no security leak, no enemy penetration, no betrayal or defection would occur that would force his recall to Moscow.

Razin punctuated our chief's monologue with the

clip of a nail clipper as he trimmed his fingernails. My stomach turned in revulsion at the sight of his nail parings falling on the green baize table.

'. . . Naturally it is difficult to analyse the strategy of the American intelligence operatives and their directors in Washington. . .' Chervenkov was saying in his burly voice. 'With repeated dismissals, personnel changes, and exposé articles published by their disaffected agents for lucrative profit, Central Intelligence headquarters out at Langley in Virginia is plainly a morass.'

This was standard Chervenkov. Paint the enemy in blackest hues and slander him as incompetent. However, if the Americans did not pose a direct threat to Chervenkov and Soviet activities in Austria this meeting would never have been convened. I waited to find out the point, what it was all about.

'. . . Thus clearly, to detract from their failures, American intelligence has mounted an offensive against Soviet personnel. The attempt to suborn our code clerk last evening was only the latest in a despicable string of provocations.' At this stage, like a star pupil in drama class, Chervenkov slapped a heavy manila file with the palm of his hand.

'Paris. London. Bonn. Within the past month there have been three attempts to compromise or recruit Soviet personnel.'

'What you are saying,' the Ambassador quickly intervened to maintain his nominal primacy, 'is that we must anticipate a further attempt to penetrate embassy security in Vienna.'

'There can be no penetration of embassy security in Vienna,' sneered Razin.

'Is that a fact, *Tovarishch* Razin?' I interjected. 'Thus you guarantee that never again will one of our trusted code clerks walk down Boltzmanngasse to waiting black Citroen automobiles?'

Furious, Razin gnawed at his fingernails with his rodent-like teeth.

'Had I personally conducted that operation last night on Boltzmanngasse—'

'Then our code clerk would now be receiving generous doses of Amytal and LSD inside the American embassy.'

'I must protest at these insinuations from a member of the staff who—'

'Who returned your code official.'

I so dislike this little Stalinist. Razin's concept of intelligence was unchanged from the days of basement interrogations and mass roundups. With people like him around, it is no wonder my service is still slandered in Anglo-Saxon espionage films.

We traded a few more nasty remarks which drew Chervenkov's mediation.

'Sergei, Razin, cease this mutual recrimination,' he commanded. 'Comrade Razin continues to bear our confidence that any attempted penetration by the Americans will be unmasked. But that is not the primary purpose of this conference. It is my contention that we have not the luxury to wait in a defensive attitude for the next intrigue directed against this embassy. The record shows it is the Americans who have deliberately intensified their provocations. I argue that they can be deterred only by direct offensive operations.'

The Ambassador glanced up from his ball-point-pen hexagons.

'I warn you that Austrian neutrality can in no way be violated.'

'This is a working assumption, Ambassador. However, our task is relatively straightforward. First, we must determine which American intelligence organisation is vulnerable to our counter-operations. Second, we must exploit that vulnerability to the utmost.'

'What do you conceive?' snapped the Ambassador. 'Do you want to drag the Americans into a scandal? Or force them to recall one of their agents?'

'The exact nature of the operation is for us now to decide. But I intend to devise an action which will be distasteful and unacceptable to the US intelligence representatives in the city of Vienna. When the Americans discover that their obnoxious practices are repaid by pain, and my definition of pain is a broad one extending to embarrassment and defamation, then they should cease their schemes against us.'

'Thus,' I added, 'our first requirement is to designate which American we are going to hurt.'

'Precisely,' Chervenkov the *Rezident* replied. 'Then we define how we are going to hurt him.'

Chapter 3

Three hours later we stopped for tea and cold sandwiches. The security cell's damnable air conditioning, supposedly manufactured by our finest Soviet craftsmen, spluttered and wheezed. The Ambassador wiped perspiration from his heavy face, removed his coat and unbuttoned his vest. That was the signal for the rest of us. I stripped off my coat and rolled up my sweaty shirtsleeves.

Razin had begun to smoke his foul cigarettes. The scent of stale tobacco burned my nostrils. Water vapour, trapped inside the humid plastic box, condensed on the sides of our container. I watched moodily as the plexiglass walls began to sweat. Then through the tepid air I sniffed the scent of perfume. A wave of disgust wrenched my stomach. It was Razin, the *muzhik*. Peasant.

Soviet society, I should explain, enjoying the blessings of centralised direction by five-year plans, is granted one universal brand of scent which serves as perfume for the ladies, after-shave lotion for the gentlemen, and deodorant for just about everybody. To a Westerner this sounds far-fetched, but by God it's the truth!

Imagine my shock when I first confronted British and American television commercials advertising a dozen brands of after-shave lotion. Compare such luxury to the ubiquitous scent-plus-shaving lotion distributed throughout the length and breadth of the USSR! More revolting, imagine the plump Mrs Razin, arising from her slumbers, dabbing a touch of scent on her fat throat while her husband Comrade Razin slaps the same sticky lotion on his razor-nicked face!

'. . . The principal question is, what of the CIA personnel inside the American embassy?' Chervenkov rapped his tea glass with an aluminium spoon.

'They have barricaded themselves inside,' someone spoke up. 'Obviously they panicked after last night's failure.'

'Where are the wives?'

'Three families were evacuated to the United States.'

'Eh. *Before* the attempt. They try to reduce their vulnerability.'

'The CIA expects some sort of reaction from us,' said Razin.

'A difficult target—'

'Then we change our target. Find another American intelligence group in Vienna.'

'Why do we speak of other groups?' interrupted the Ambassador. 'All of these people ultimately are paid from Washington.'

'This refers,' injected Chervenkov, 'to something they have here called, uh. . .' he leafed through his thick file, '. . . uh, the "I" Board.'

'The I Board?'

'It is an American abbreviation. For "Joint Intelligence Operations Board".'

'There are too many Washington bureaucrats,' grumbled the Ambassador. 'NSA. CIA. I Board. Why don't you lump together the damn lot? One American espionage operative is the same as another, no?'

I waited impatiently through all these preliminaries. I knew what the I Board was. That was why Chervenkov waved in my direction for an explanation.

'Sergei?'

I rose and placed my fingertips on the green-baize tablecloth.

'The so-called I Board is a product of American administrative confusion. Several years ago a decision was taken by the president that a clearing board was necessary to sift their intelligence. They were drowning in red tape, computer prints, and contingency studies from, among others, the CIA, State Department intelligence, the National Security Agency of Fort Meade, Maryland, and the Defense Intelligence Agency at the Pentagon in Arlington, Virginia.'

'You speak as though you know Arlington in Virginia,' sniffed Razin.

'I know Virginia very well, *Tovarishch*,' smiling at his attempt to distract me. 'The new Joint Intelligence Operations Board was established in Roslyn, Virginia. Vis à vis the District of Columbia across the Francis Scott Key bridge. Its mission was to rationalise the flow of intelligence documents to the American president.'

'They were to consolidate reports from all these other organisations, to stop the in-fighting. All those agencies were pushing each other like pigs eating corn husks.'

'Predictably,' I continued, 'knowing American government bureaucracy, the I Board merely *expanded* the volume of paperwork. And it immediately burrowed itself into choice assignments overseas. Particularly London, Paris, Bonn and Vienna.'

'Where in Vienna?'

'In a cover office on Gunoldstrasse.'

'Nineteenth district—'

'The I Board's cover is a fictitious involvement in East–West commerce. They act as though employed in East–West leasing operations and management consulting.'

The discussion quickly became bogged down in explanations about the Vienna I Board. Who was in charge? What was their budget? What kind of automobiles did they drive? To what extent did they operate at cross purposes to the Central Intelligence Agency?

'The Vienna I Board director is called Leslie Stillwater,' explained Chervenkov. 'From the American state of Texas.'

Razin interrupted.

'I have once seen this man. Fat and plump, with little sense of dress. . .' as though Razin were Beau Brummell, '. . . very strange style and with freckles on his nose.'

'One should add for Comrade Razin,' I continued, 'that Mr Stillwater is a graduate of the Massachusetts Institute of Technology and served with the US Atomic Energy Agency. He is not quite the Texas yokel you wish us to believe.'

Razin began impaling cigarette butts on the tip of his pencil:

'Since you are thus well informed, perhaps you will advise on the means of implementing Comrade Chervenkov's directive to combat the Americans.'

This was a tricky little ploy. Chervenkov raised his barbed-wire eyebrows and stared in my direction for a proposal.

I again rose, but not as quickly as previously.

'First we must define our strengths as Russians,' I began steadily. 'Then we need to evaluate the weaknesses of our American opposition. Essentially we Russians are consequential. A key element of our training is to act in logical sequence. Sudden impulses should not be allowed to disrupt detailed planning.'

I deliberately began in this fashion, not only because I believed every word of what I said, but also because I wanted to draw this interminable meeting to an end.

'The Americans, on the contrary, are impulsive. Their intelligence officers are beset by the whims of fickle public opinion. One year, for example, they glorify an ethic of public honesty. The next they may revert to the most obnoxious and horrible acts of defamation and assassination. This is why they are so dangerous. Because they are so impulsive they create great damage and wreckage, even when all we might seek is to leave them alone, live and let live.'

'I notice,' spat out Razin, 'that they were consequential enough to place cosmonauts on the moon. Before us.'

'It illustrates my point. The Americans devoted enormous emotion and expense to conquer space. But they could not channel similar emotion and expense to conquer the organised crime and addictions which drain the equivalent cost of their space programme from their economy.'

Razin was trying to rattle me. Dull beats of pressure throbbed at my temples. My eyes stung with the bad air and stench from his cigarettes. I tried to breathe regularly and fight against the tension he provoked. Don't knot up, I told myself. Say it slowly and directly and get it done:

'The remainder is very straightforward. The CIA mob have bolted and put themselves behind closed doors. They are out of our reach. The employees of the I Board? They are out in the open, exposed, but their chief, Stillwater, is incorruptible.'

'Then find one of the I Board bastards who is corruptible!' Chervenkov growled.

'That is exactly what I propose.' From my briefcase

I extracted seven copies of the I Board dossier which I passed to my colleagues around the table.

'His name is Westfall.'

'Westfall. You know this Westfall?'

'Following directives, I play volleyball against him each Thursday evening.'

Chervenkov studied the documents for a very long while. Time passed wearily. Finally he shifted his bulk, stared in my direction and made a decision:

'We want him hurt, Sergei. We want him ruined. You develop the specifics and the tactics and inform me later of the details. It is immaterial if this Westfall comes crawling in the mud, or is sentenced for ten years by the Austrians, or deported by his own officials to an American penitentiary. Take your time, proceed carefully, be very patient, but hurt this Westfall as an example to the others. So that never again will these Anglo-Saxons put a finger on a Soviet official under my jurisdiction. Can you guarantee that?'

A tear of sweat poised to trickle down the side of the plexiglass compartment. Quietly, Razin leaned back in his chair and looked at me contentedly. He seemed pleased that I had assumed the complete burden of Chervenkov's proposal. If I accepted it. A negative reply would have been sufficient. But after my profession of faith in Soviet logical analysis a negative answer would have been hypocritical.

'Yes, I guarantee it.'

Shortly after that the meeting adjourned.

Much later that evening I unlocked our apartment door and was met by clacking typewriter keys. I went into the study and kissed the little freckles on the back of Olga's neck. She didn't look up from her desk.

'What time is tomorrow evening at the Bulgarians?' she said, rummaging for the plastic bottle of white fluid that blots out typewriter errors.

'Five forty-five.'

'Your invitation card said five-thirty.'

'With the Bulgarians, a Soviet official can afford to be fifteen minutes late.' I sank into a plastic armchair.

We were discussing a reception at the Bulgarian embassy on Schwindgasse to promote their Plovdiv trade fair. Because of the work on her dissertation Olga had instructed our receptionist to forward her regrets. I was required to show up.

'I will get you something to drink.'

We both knew that the next evening I faced three hours drinking sticky Bulgarian cognac. I told her it wasn't necessary to get up.

She must have worked at the desk throughout the day, I thought tiredly. This morning I had awakened and placed the flat of my hand on the warm bedclothes where she had been sleeping. Then it was that I heard the click of her typewriter in the little study.

Now, slumped in the chair after the endless meeting in the security cell I watched the woman who had shared virtually all of my professional life. It would be unfair to call Olga heavy, for she was strong-boned and equally tall as I and carried her weight handsomely. She was exceptionally fair, with soft blonde hair which she wore short now, and white skin which in summer shaded into a pale rosy hue. This reminded me of the heroines in nineteenth-century English novels I had read at the university. When we first met as students her hair grew long and flowing, but she had it cut just before Anatoli was born. For years I had jokingly complained against its short length, and now we had reached a compromise where it brushed the nape of her neck.

Olga's face was narrow and fortunately lacked the puffy fleshiness of so many Russians. With her distant, grey-flecked eyes she was a good-looking woman, despite my complaints about her short hair. In the past I had been compelled to address curt words to colleagues who paid her excessive, undiplomatic attention. Attention which she by no means encouraged. Olga is not unfaithful to me – unless I have been cuckolded by her devotion to the doctoral thesis on models of Soviet economic planning.

My rivals grumble over the fact that my early marriage to Olga did no harm to my career. They constantly dredge up the name of her father to account for my overseas assignments and promotions.

I make no secret of the fact that my father-in-law Dipl. Ing. G. V. Sokolovskiy is Soviet Minister of Petroleum and Mining. *Ex officio* this makes him a cabinet minister. Even more significant, he is a member of the Central Committee of the Communist Party of the Soviet Union. My enemies draw the conclusion that I am my father-in-law's protégé.

I enjoy the company of, and am devoted to, Ing. Sokolovskiy, but I won't dignify such accusations with further discussion. He would not remain a member of the Central Committee if he stooped to pull strings for his son-in-law.

'Papa's picture was in the *Financial Times*,' Olga called out as I wandered into the other room and switched on the TV.

'Why are you reading the *Financial Times*?'

'Because Papa had his picture in it.'

'Why do the British write about your father?'

The screen wiggled to life. A heavy Austrian matron was talking about packaged soup.

'Because he is selling them petroleum their rivals can't buy.'

'. . . *und schmeckt wunderbar*!' the lady lapped soup out of a spoon.

'What rivals? They are all in a petroleum cartel!'

'Cut it down! Not when he gives British Petroleum a seven per cent discount the Americans don't get!'

This was all meaningless to me.

I watched through dried soups, and women's spray deodorant, floor polish, nasal squirt and oven cleaner before the balding Austrian news announcer took over.

Olga slammed down the typewriter cover and padded into the living room in her slippers.

'Green and blue?' I said, noticing for the first time her green synthetic fibre blouse and blue acrylic skirt.

'It's for working at the desk, dear,' she said tightly. 'Were I going to your Bulgarian cocktail party I would be more matching.'

We sat through thirty minutes of complaints about unbalanced budgets and new taxes, and the tourism industry didn't like the rainy weather. Then she cooked supper and we watched an inane Austrian quiz show and she went to bed a lot earlier than I did.

Chapter 4

The so-called sidewalk café of the Hotel Imperial on the ring is cramped and noisy, but when I had telephoned Westfall, he said we should meet there and I suppose it reflects his questionable taste. I am continually amazed by the Americans' lack of breeding on the one hand and their attraction to the pretentious on the other. When I was stationed in Washington I noticed that half the congressmen from Kansas and Iowa frequented restaurants called Chez Pierre.

He said one o'clock but I wanted to get there ahead of him. I settled back and watched the dense traffic. Mercedes and dented Volkswagens and Opels poured onto the Ringstrasse from Schwarzenbergplatz honking illegally and beeping and fouling the air. The Roman-columned *historismus* façades along the ring quivered in the exhaust fumes.

Tram bells jingled cheerfully and young Britishers and Americans with backpacks hurried around the corner to McDonalds hamburgers while three Arabs in white robes walked into Austrian Airlines. A bearded man in clogs set up a portable table and handed out leaflets protesting against nuclear electricity generation while a chinless Austrian executive in a roll brim hat attempted to discover who had backed into the direction light of his Mercedes 280 CE.

At the entrance to the Imperial, workmen had begun to assemble ornamental guard boxes and I noticed the plain-clothes security officials conferring with traffic police. Another itinerant head of state was due to arrive at the hotel. The neutral Austrians had turned state visits into a major money-making industry. A van stopped in front of the hotel and labourers struggled to emplace two mammoth potted evergreen trees beside the red and white striped guard boxes. It looked like a set from *The Merry Widow*.

I reviewed what I knew of this man Westfall. Like me, he was in his middle thirties, but I trusted that there the similarities stopped. He was no professional. Hired by the I Board on local contract. At loose ends in Europe for ten years. Smattering of five languages, fluent in none of them. He had been involved in automobile transactions which were little more than common theft. I suppose Stillwater, the Vienna I Board chief, used his police record as leverage to keep him disciplined. I would have to look elsewhere for a pressure point.

Girls? Westfall had a weakness for Balkan girls. He was always seen running around with Yugoslav or Romanian women.

Armed? Not in Vienna. But there was an unconfirmed report that in the snow outside Innsbruck he had killed a *West* German agent. We never received all the details because it was a squalid intra-NATO vendetta. Apparently Westfall had been struck in the face with a shotgun stock and broke the agent's neck with a pistol butt.

He had initiated the contact with me in Vienna, undoubtedly under instruction from Stillwater. That had been most useful as far as I was concerned and was particularly appropriate now that he was my target.

I took reverse bearings and analysed what he knew of me. Nothing. Hearsay. Gossip. Undoubtedly his dossiers were full of reports on my assignments in the UK and Washington. But what reports? My behaviour had been impeccable. To all observers I had been nothing more than an assistant economics attaché.

And so I would continue to be, as I now prepared for Westfall's arrival. I watched one of my embassy technicians browsing at the newspaper kiosk across from the Imperial café. As soon as he verified Westfall's arrival, he and two other specialists would initiate a survey of his apartment.

We, the watchers, wanted to know if Westfall was having his own place watched. It was my intention to wire that flat from top to bottom, but not if Westfall was going to have us photographed as we wired it.

A D-tram rattled to a halt by the kiosk. The embassy technician plucked a copy of *Newsweek* from the rack. Inside the tram a tall man kissed a girl with very long black hair, pressing her shoulder, then he swung on the rails and landed on the pavement. I put on my sunglasses. The technician waved his magazine and opened the door of a waiting taxi. I leaned back as Westfall walked in my direction.

'Hi Sergei!' he yelled.

'Hello Wes,' I said in English.

Westfall was some four or five centimetres taller than I and I'm not squat. He was rawboned, long and lanky. Originally from some interior province of the United States, he had been in Europe so long that numerous continental traits had been superimposed on his corn-pone mannerisms. He was wearing Italian sandals, American Levi jeans, and a blue French Lacoste shirt with a little crocodile over his pectoral muscle.

He was dark haired and sunburned. Several months previously he had flourished a beard, but this had now been trimmed back into an inappropriate, if neatly clipped, RAF-style Battle of Britain moustache.

There was a hook scar across his cheekbone. I gathered that this was from the shotgun stock. Someone had scarred the back of his right hand with a cigarette.

'Who's the pretty girl?'

'Ah, Sergei,' Westfall grinned and yelled in atrocious German for a draught beer, 'paragraph 27, page 232 of your interrogation manual: "An agent's first objective is to verify the romantic attachments of his quarry." *Nicht wahr*?'

I chuckled somewhat uneasily. He continually teased me of alleged involvement in intelligence activity, hoping to draw outraged denials. It was a ham-handed tactic, but it could make me squirm, particularly since fifty people sitting around the sidewalk tables had heard him bellow it out.

'There is volleyball tonight.'

'Not me! No more!'

'No more?'

'You Russians on the team are too arrogant. You never feed me the ball.'

'Well then, how are you going to exercise?'

'I'll exercise. Don't think you get so much strain with your bloody volleyball. Look at that paunch you've started. For a tall man like you you should be ashamed.'

'I have no paunch!' but I glanced at my waistline.

Two German girls in identical white hip-hugging jeans and sun halters had stopped on the sidewalk beside our table. They were trying to find the Belvedere gallery on their map of Vienna.

Westfall bounded to his feet and addressed them to the effect, I-donta-spreck-German-but-my-friend-here-he-is-most-fluent, pointing at me.

I had no choice but to stand and make a little nod.

'*Bitte, Gnädiges Fräulein*?'

'Ask them to sit down and drink beer!' Westfall hissed in a stage whisper.

Politely I explained they should take the D-tram up Prinz Eugenstrasse to the palace entrance. One of the girls hesitated as she looked up from under her mascara and I noted the outline of a bikini brassière on her tanned shoulders.

'We go to the Belvedere gallery to study the Gustav Klimts.'

'There are many Gustav Klimts in the gallery,' I agreed.

'The suave European gentleman,' Westfall teased as I watched the girls walk toward the tram stop.

'Of course I am European. We Russians are not tribesmen from the Fiji Islands.'

'You think you are a cultured European, but your dress and manners are as slovenly as a Turk.'

'Oh come come, Wes! You are simply jealous.' That remark about my clothing stung my vanity. After my residence in London I rather prided myself on my ability to choose good suits of clothes.

'Where'd you get that sports jacket? Looks like something from the basement of the Kleiderhaus.' Westfall was referring to a mass-produced clothing outlet.

'I bought this on the Kärntnerstrasse,' Vienna's most expensive shopping street. But in truth it came from a department store on the Kärntnerstrasse.

Westfall dug a business card from his jeans pocket.

'Try my tailor.' He flipped the dog-eared card across the table.

Heinz Mohr, the card was engraved. I knew the address. It was a fashionable establishment, which specialised in hand-crafted suits for doctors, judges and the odd *Graf* here and there. Westfall was clearly teasing me: I couldn't remember ever having seen him wear a necktie.

We leaned back, drank a beer, traded gibes and watched the flow of people on the sidewalk.

'You should loosen up, Sergei. Follow your emotion and impulses. By now you could be showing those German girls the wonders of the Belvedere gardens!'

'As usual you mix your directives. Emotion and impulse are completely separate nervous phenomena. I am as emotional as the next man. But I am not impulsive, since I believe it is civilised to govern one's impulses.'

'*Naja*. It don't float. You think of yourself as a rational individual in control of your urges. In reality you are at the mercy of appetites and impulses of which you are scarcely aware.'

'No no!' I laughed excitedly. The waitress passed by and I ordered more beer. 'You Americans are the ones who are fickle. Look at your consumer society. It's based totally on impulsive purchasing. We are the ones who at least attempt to run a society in a coherent fashion.'

'Stop mixing up people and Society with a capital S!'

'Well, we, not you, provide a rational framework.'

'Your almighty five-year plan? Buddy, no thanks!'

'Our planning is imperfect because the people who administer it may be imperfect. But events with us are predictable. Objectives are defined in advance, which is not the case with you. You improvise. You are pushed by impulses created for you by television announcers or events which you do not anticipate and thus not control.'

'OK. We will see,' he shrugged, spinning a cork beer mat on the table top. 'Tell me something, Sergei.'

'Anything you ask.'

'Is Moscow Dynamo football team really subsidised by the KGB?'

'What!'

Typically, he had sprung from the philosophical to the banal. I struggled to keep my balance.

'Some sports writer in the London *Observer* says all Soviet teams with Dynamo in their name are on the KGB payroll.'

'Now, why would the KGB subsidise football teams?'

'To win football games, why do you think they subsidise them?'

In fact, I must admit that my service has been known to channel monies to teams called Dynamo.

'Well,' I chuckled jovially, 'I think it's somewhat more complicated than that,' not answering the question.

'It's Thursday night tonight, Sergei. Go out there and play volleyball with your other Russkies and get exercise for your tummy.'

'The only exercise I am going to get is eating Bulgarian sandwiches and drinking their liquors.'

'The occupational hazards of the young diplomat on the cocktail circuit.'

'I have no occupational hazards.'

'Oh no?'

'No.'

'No?'

Now, looking back on that sidewalk chat, how much wiser it would have been to admit, yes, yes, Wes, both of us have hazards.

Humidity boiled through the baroque windows of the Bulgarian embassy on Schwindgasse as two hundred commercial attachés and their womenfolk gorged on suckling pig, *kebab*, *cevapcici* and *sarmi*. Men gnawed postage-stamp slivers of toast and gooseliver while balancing china plates overloaded with Westphalian ham. Butlers in wilted white jackets bulldozed through the mob with trays of Bulgarian cognac, slivovica, *cherveno vino*, stupefying *mastika*, Campari soda, Jim Beam and Crimean champagne.

Around the buffet table pressed North Koreans in high-necked black tunics, Italians in impeccable white linen, sweating Bulgarian security men in open-necked shirts and seventy-five obese Austrians in identical blue suits. A demure Pakistani economics official was explaining the mysteries of cricket to a Czech foreign trade director, some Yugoslav was reminding the Irish ambassador that Bulgaria had no legal claim to Yugoslav Macedonia, and a West German banker was politely declining an invitation to spend his vacation on the glorious Black Sea coast.

The women were munching away and holding their own. There was the resplendent blonde wife of the French consul in a diaphanous white Emilio Pucci creation, stocky-limbed German *Hausfraus*, a Polish minister's wife sweating through the armpits of her mauve evening dress, and swarthy Hungarian ladies one step away from the gypsy campfire and tambourine act.

Unfortunately, I had been button-holed by a director of Sofia's Balkancarexport. Balkancarexport, I was reminded, was the world's leading exporter of fork-lift trucks, which it was now selling in West Germany, the director emphasised proudly as he gurgled more cognac. It was very significant. I certainly agreed, failing to mention that when the West Germans bought these fork-lift machines they blasted off the paint, overhauled the engines, stamped the direction lettering in English, rust-proofed the frames, and relined the brakes. Balkancar exports were ever growing, the director beamed and I said how right he was. Was I attending the Plovdiv fair to see the Balkancar exhibit in September? Why, there was nowhere else in Europe I wanted to be. *Au revoir* Paris, Florence, Monte Carlo, Venice and Amsterdam.

I was being lectured on the new fork-lift hydraulic mechanism when she walked in, blinked at the sweaty air, and strode to the window. She didn't grab a drink tray or start spearing beef chunks. She smiled, shook her head and declined to chat with a matador-thin Spanish diplomat, and stood there and watched the feeding act.

I can recall many impressions from that moment, but beyond all I remember those long, tapered coltish legs, the wonderful athletic tautness of her smoothed muscles. Her body moved with the total unselfconscious ease of a young girl who has just discovered she has become an exceedingly pretty young woman. She wore white satin hose and a free flowing blue cotton dress open to expose a sinuous dark throat. She was excessively dark, virtually bronzed, with long, jet black hair, and oval Mediterranean brown eyes that spoke of olive oil and southern sea and cypress.

We Russians have no modern expressions for encounters of this nature. Leave it to the Americans and Hollywood or their television, but they do come forth with the phrases. Chills up the spine and someone across crowded rooms, I saw her standing there and all at once it was you.

Daria.

Her name was Daria. She was the daughter of the Bulgarian ambassador, Kaladzhiev.

When I had seen her last it had been three years ago and she had been twenty. She had just arrived with her father from Sofia and was clad virtually in a peasant skirt and kerchief. *Bozhe*, I said, peasant girl no longer, watching her lean back against the wainscoting with a bored, ironic smile on her tight lips. Then she turned and showed a Byzantine profile that men climbed into ships and launched fleets for.

I knew I could then perform one of two acts. I could continue listening to the superior achievements of Balkancar fork-lift trucks. Or I could walk across the room to Daria.

'I am Sergei,' bowing stiffly and taking her hand. 'Several years have passed—'

'*Priyatno*!' she said cheerfully in Russian. 'How's Olga and your son Anatoli?'

My neck snapped back and I turned to grasp a vodka from the passing waiter.

'My compliments to your father on the successful reception for—'

'Hey, lean over here,' she laughed.

'Yes?'

'Personally, this is a crashing bore,' she whispered. 'Pardon me, but it's purely *gavno*,' our Russian equivalent of the four-letter Anglo-Saxon scatological noun.

She stared at me gravely with those brown eyes, then we both started giggling.

'Mademoiselle Kaladzhieva, *enchanté*!' burst in the French commercial counsellor, planting on Daria's brown hand a wet Gallic kiss.

Very tersely in her best Bulgarian Daria lied that she understood not one word of French. He mumbled a few *desolés* and backed off to chase the Italian consul's wife.

'*Dvizheniye*,' meaning too much automobile traffic, she shrugged her lithe shoulders. 'You didn't answer my question.'

'Anatoli is in Moscow. He is now thirteen but, my word, he is growing quickly for his age. Our fear is that they will advance him too fast in the hockey competition. He must develop self-confidence, improve his skating with the puck and passing.'

Daria looked up with those dark, fresco eyes and let me ramble. I never mentioned Olga and she did not press me to do so.

'Please fetch me an *hors d'oeuvre*,' suddenly refluent in French.

'Get them yourself, it's your party.'

She walked away and I was not certain she would come back to me. I hunched my shoulders. It was something that had to be established. Magically, the press parted at the table, Daria stepped forward and accepted a tiny plate with slices of smoked salmon. She received a glass of white wine, spoke to several of the Bulgarians, paused briefly, and returned to me at the open window.

'Surprised?' she smiled.

'I was verifying what sort of education you have received over the past three years.'

'It hasn't been a Swiss finishing school. That what you mean?'

'That is not what I mean.'

'My father sent me to the University of Vienna where I finished my 'laureat. For the past year I have been at the beaux arts academy in Munich.'

Ambassador Kaladzhiev is a member of the Central Committee of the Bulgarian Communist Party, I thought rapidly. *Previously served as secretary for information. Former editor of Sofia's* Rabotnichesko Delo. *Routine counterintelligence reports favourable on his service in Vienna. Main line party member.*

‘Munich. You certainly did not choose the squalid dregs of Europe.’

‘I chose a place I could learn something about photography.’ She tapped her glass with a long fingernail. ‘Now don’t be boring and tell me that *all* daughters of Bulgarian party officials do nothing but study photography and cinema.’

‘I won’t tell you that, but it happens to be true.’

‘That shouldn’t stop me from doing it? Do you know how long I had to work to pay for my Nikon? Daddy wouldn’t pay a *stotinki*.’

‘How are you going to employ your new artistic skills within the Peoples’ Republic of Bulgaria?’

‘It’s completely unimportant. They can send me to work at the textile mills.’

The crowd had ebbed back from the buffet table and nearly crushed her against me in the heat. I looked down on her and scented her perfume of citron and lime. My throat tightened in dryness. It was extremely foolish to be seen speaking with her for such a protracted length of time. Two other Soviets were in the crowd. Her bronzed image flickered in the evening light, precisely crafted white teeth, dark lashed eyes. The embassy economists. Curving, sinuous throat to the point of her breasts. The vodka glass felt lukewarm in my hand. Set it down. Dark breasts. . . . The official from Balkancar was speaking with a Hungarian intelligence official. Grunting and swilling sounds rushed around me. I breathed shallow in the heat. My tongue parched from the warm vodka. . .

‘I would rather not continue chit-chatting like this.’

‘That is up to you, Sergei. As the Americans say,’ switching into English, ‘the ball is now in your field.’

‘Court.’

‘Then?’

'It would be very important to meet.'

'Why that is wonderful. Have the Soviet limousine deliver you and your wife Olga to the Bulgarian embassy.'

'NO,' I said, the palms of my hands sweating with tension. 'No.'

She sipped white wine and looked at me for a very long while.

'Very good then. Shall we say the University? On the Ring. At twelve noon tomorrow. Is that clandestine enough, Counsellor?' and walked toward the Italians.

Two hours afterward from the public telephone booth in the Karlsplatz metro station I telephoned a reserve number at my embassy.

'You are now secure,' the duty clerk noted after I had allowed the tone to ring for two minutes' duration.

'Preliminary.'

'*Da*?'

'Bulgarian subject.'

'Proceed.'

'Kaladzhieva. Daria.'

I hung up the receiver, entered a neon-lit espresso bar and drank a cup of coffee fouled by the stale air. In thirty minutes I returned to the booth and called the embassy line.

'Kaladzhieva. Daria', I said.

'Father, Bulgarian ambassador. Consequently, official permission granted for study and temporary residence in West. No prejudicial activity yet recorded,' replied the intelligence clerk who had just run a check on Daria through the embassy's Honeywell computer. '*Chistaya*.'

Or, clean as a whistle if I were to translate it into Anglo-American.

Chapter 5

Drumming my fingers on the formica table I listened to the technician Syzmanski catalogue his little safari into Westfall's apartment.

'. . . Entry at 14:05,' he droned. 'Complicated uh double action lock, you know on all these old Viennese doors, uh, the keys weigh like blocks of lead. . .'

'I am not concerned with the weight of Westfall's keys!' I snapped. 'You were not to enter unless certain the place was not under observation!'

'There's nothing across the street.'

'What do you mean there's nothing across the street!'

Monotonously, Syzmanski explained that Westfall's flat on the Untere Viaduct Strasse faced an elevated stone viaduct carrying the tram line across the Danube canal.

Syzmanski reeked of sardines. I have seen the man eat five cans at one sitting. Paunchy, roly poly, with thin blond hair and a tiny loden hat perched on his head, he was actually a White Russian from Minsk. He spoke Russian, Polish and German. This made him indispensable for backstairs assignments in Austria since he was instantly accepted as a Viennese. His name caused no problem. If one thinks that all citizens of Vienna are called Schmidt or Bauer then check the telephone directory: half the burgers listed therein are named Czerny, Jelinek, Nowotny, Svoboda or Zdrazil.

'The hallway is knocked through a brick wall,' stated Syzmanski. 'There is no adjoining apartment which could be employed as a, uh, listening base.'

'You guarantee that, do you Syzmanski?'

With a wave of sardine breath Syzmanski told me he guaranteed it.

Twelve o'clock. It was essential to meet Daria at the university at twelve o'clock. No! Earlier! I had to drive through the traffic and park before twelve o'clock! Would not Syzmanski terminate this account of Westfall's apartment? By God, it was already eleven and the man was mumbling about wax impressions of Westfall's keys! I had to stop this. . . Get the report written. . . Get out of the embassy on time. . . Twelve o'clock. . .

'. . . We decided to do a standard cut-out on his telephone wires,' he continued with all the enthusiasm of the technician.

'*Da da*, go on!'

'You understand what a cut-out—'

'Of course I understand! You used the existing wires of his telephone. To bug the instrument and run the broadcast to a separate transmitter. What about a wall receiver?'

'Here, *vot vot*,' tapping a rough sketch of Westfall's flat. 'A centralised point was—'

'*Da*. Good. I understand. Don't spell it out.'

'—implanted in the base of the table lamp, located here.'

'Wires?' Twelve noon, if. . .

'*Vot*. Baseboard. To the telephone. Then joint wires running to outside terminal in the hallway here,' tap tap on the diagram. To get away. I had to get away. . . Twelve. . .

'The VHF transmitter. We installed it in the access duct to the hallway.'

'Where it will be discovered by the Austrian postal authorities!' Idiots! To get away. . .

'The metal case was rusted shut and the seal read. 1941. It has never been controlled. The Austrian postal administration are lazy pigs.' He burped essence of sardine oil and scratched his fat neck.

'*Zdravstvuy Amerikanets*!'

It was security-chief Razin, popping his rat-like head into my office.

'Success in your venture?' he whined.

Get the hell out of here you little rodent, I started to shout.

'Why, good morning, Razin,' I smiled.

'How does it all progress?'

'How does what all progress?'

'Ah *Amerikanets*, always answer a question with another question, no?'

Amerikanets, or, 'the American', was the tag Razin had gratuitously pinned on me. This reflected his jealousy of my assignments in London and Washington, and my ability when required to express myself in proper English syntax. In his bigoted mind, I suppose, I had adopted far too many mannerisms of the opposition.

'You see, Razin,' I continued, 'it was not my understanding that this assignment was open to public scrutiny.'

'Westfall has a lot of books lying around,' said Syzmanski the technician. 'Here's the photographs we made of the place.'

'Anything involving Westfall involves my counter-intelligence,' Razin spat out.

'. . . a girl's been in there. Pair of girl's jeans and electric hair-dryer, bathrobe, and some red nail-polish.'

'What did the jeans label read?'

'. . . in addition, a highly unprofessional, provocative entrance into the man's apartment,' complained

Razin. 'You will not receive support from me if you are jailed by the Austrian police!'

'. . . it's here in my notebook,' answered Syzmanski, paying no attention to Razin. 'Jeans label, it says *Robna Kuča Beograd*. What's that?'

'Belgrade department store. Westfall's running around with a Yugoslav girl.' It was now 11:20. Razin. I had to get rid of Razin. I could never finish with the technical report if Razin continued to pry into my operation. 11:22. I had until twelve o'clock. I clenched my fists, uncoiled my fingers, clenched my fists and felt sticky sweat on my palms. Daria. Daria Kaladzhieva. I was not going to lose the opportunity to meet Daria because of the rodent-like Razin. . .

'He's got an old phonograph apparatus in there,' droned on Syzmanski. 'There are some scratched records of strange American singers called, uh it says here, Hank Williams who plays something looking like one of our mandolins and wears a cowboy hat. . .'

'Now Sergei,' leered Razin, 'you the American expert will proceed to lecture us on the famous country singer Hank Williams and his contribution to North American folklore. . .'

'What else, quick.'

'Uh, records. Somebody called Corel-li.'

'Then? Hurry!'

'Pur-ce-ll. Er, Dow-ling. Al-bi-non-i. And a big set of Bach records apparently he bought in Bucharest, Romania.'

'The son of a bitch probably knew you were coming,' Razin sneered. 'Tried to make himself impressive.'

'Syzmanski, please be so kind as to leave the office for three minutes.'

'Yes sir,' he got up and waddled out to the corridor.

'Giving orders, Sergei?'

I turned around in my swivel chair and faced the man squarely.

'Comrade Razin, my operational instructions are to conduct a punitive assignment against the American I Board agent, Westfall. Such instructions contain no statement that I am to be supervised, lectured, pried into or spied upon by officials of this embassy. If you wish, at this moment we will seek modification of said instructions from the *Rezident*. If not, leave my office. You are an unwanted intrusion into matters of my concern.'

Slowly the capillaries of Razin's scalp shaded to a blood red. His pale skin flushed with heat and I sniffed his facial perfume as his pulse rose. Then without further comment he extracted the toothpick on which he had been gnawing, broke it in half, pitched it upon my desk top, and walked out of the room.

'Syzmanski!' I yelled. 'Speed it up.'

'Here's the photographs of the books.'

I studied the fuzzy black and white photograph of a pine bookshelf. Strewn about were such titles as *The Battle of Mons*, *The First Day on the Somme*, *The Way of a Trout with a Fly*, *Attacking Rugby*, Vol de Nuit and *Humphry Clinker*.

'A complete mish-mash! Probably hasn't read one of them!'

'The man's writing a story.'

'What's that?'

'We took photographs of the uncompleted manuscript. If you can read his terrible handwriting.'

I studied the demented scrawl of a functional illiterate. 'The Duel', he called it. Italian riviera. A playboy. His mistress. An Italian doctor. A big business executive. Well Ho! Ho! Unfortunately for the would-be author Westfall I immediately recognised that he was plagiarising Chekhov's greatest short story of the same title.

'Listen then, Syzmanski, are you impressed with our Westfall?'

'The bastard's a spy. You say so and we take him down to the Danube. He doesn't impress me.'

No, no, but who was this man? Was it all a carefully concocted front? Had there been any means of his learning we would force his apartment? How far could he stage-manage his own incidentals, the scraps of one's life left around an empty apartment? However easy it had been to penetrate the flat, my training told me to pay closer attention to penetrating Westfall's role, if he was playing a role.

11:37.

'That's sufficient then, Syzmanski. If—'

'Sufficient? There's still the inventory of the flat to. . .'

I struggled to lock my safe with something other than breakneck haste.

'Place the inventory in the official file, which you will return to registry. Your task is now to service the telephone recordings. I want a transcript and translation of every call coming in to or out of that apartment.'

Maddeningly, with no apparent concern, he stared at me with the dull eyes of an obedient ox. Finally he shifted his weight and rose to leave the office.

'Also, I should say you have begun well. And Syzmanski,' I added, locking my desk drawer, rummaging for my car keys, 'we do not need to discuss with other officials the context of our conversation with Comrade Razin?'

'Not if you say so,' shrugging.

I almost bowled him over as I pushed through the door.

Vienna traffic at 11:46 is worse than the staccato

movement of a Prokovief symphony. Shrieks from steel tram brakes, the pulse of air compressors, the machine-gun ricochet of jackhammers ripping up asphalt trenches. I wove through a monstrous traffic jam, rushed through a red light relying on my diplomatic plates to spare me police prosecution, and roared down the ring.

11:59. There was no alternative but to double-park by the monument of the Turkish Siege across from the university. Lock the car. Hurry.

12:00. I quick-stepped through the underpass at the Schottentor and bolted for the university. Pulled on my sunglasses. Turned up the collar of my raincoat.

12:01. I reached the steps of the university. Gasped for breath. If I had only. . .

No Daria.

Clearly she was not there for me.

I stood in the grand entrance of the University of Vienna, a tall blond Russian in his thirties in a business suit and raincoat in the midst of young Austrians in Levis and Wranglers and Lee Cooper jeans, blanket ponchos and cotton-sack bookbags. I stood there twenty minutes, sweating, confused and defeated like the rawest recruit on his first day of intelligence training.

'Hey!'

'Daria!'

'Hey!' she yelled.

Chapter 6

Daria was on the other side of the ring facing the university, leaning on the hood of my limousine.

'Well come on over!' she called in English above the grind of the traffic.

Attempting to create no more attention than that I had already drawn to myself, I rushed slowly back through the Schottentor underpass and emerged at a brisk walk by my parked automobile.

Summer storm clouds, which I had not noticed in my dash to the university, were now boiling over the city and the first massive drops of rain splashed onto my windshield. Hurriedly we bolted into my Lada and drove away.

'Well hi,' she laughed as I swerved around the ring and headed down the Danube canal.

'Hello Daria.'

'Get you rattled? Did I force you to lose your composure of steel?'

'You forced me to lose my steely composure.'

Daria was in Levi jeans and an old-fashioned white linen shirt with sleeves rolled up above the elbows and shirt tail hanging out. No jewellery, bracelets, necklaces or love beads. Her long, coltish legs curved wonderfully in the tight jeans. She had undone the top three buttons of her shirt and her brown throat glistened against the linen. A Nikon camera was slung around her shoulder. She tossed it on the back seat.

I stirred uneasily in my driver's position, fighting through the Vienna traffic, attempting to escape the city centre, but constantly drawn to look at her dark-lashed eyes, throat and white teeth. Was she naked under that shirt? Was she wearing any sort of underwear? Could she be wearing a brassière? Under what pretext could I touch her shoulder? To feel a brassière strap if. . .

'First of all there is nothing to be rattled about. Second, you should concentrate on your driving and stop staring at me. That very big truck is throwing water all over your windshield.' She curled those long legs up under her and sat cross legged in the front seat. 'By the way, let's speak English, that puts us even, fifty-fifty, Bulgaro-Soviet compromise in the interest of mutual fraternal cooperation. OK?'

'It's fine'

'So what's the deal? You driving me to your hunting lodge or something?'

'I am driving you to have lunch at a restaurant beside the Danube.'

She laughed.

'With Olga and Anatoli and Daddy and you and me?'

'Just you and me. Otherwise, we would be required to do much quick telephone calling.'

'Well, let's keep away from the telephone.'

I drove on slowly through the downpour. Great sheets of rain beat on the car hood. Except for the heavy trucks, most automobiles had pulled off the highway. There would be few people driving out to the Danube restaurants. I had selected the place with considerable deliberation knowing it was well away from the restaurants normally frequented by our embassy staff, the Americans, or any inquisitive Austrian officials. In fact, it was not particularly exclusive or luxurious, but I was not in a position to dine with Daria in the main salon of the Hotel Imperial.

I pulled from the road and drove down a marshy lane reinforced with gravel and cinders. Brackish water splashed under the automobile tyres in the potholes. The long wooden boathouse which had been converted into an eating establishment loomed ahead through the rain. Heavy willow trees lashed and buckled with the wind that was ripping off the Danube. Neon lights flickered through the gloom, although it was still early in the afternoon.

Yes. Good. One or two limousines. Trucks. Not deserted. That would have been inappropriate and frightening, but it certainly was not a reservation-only situation.

I gave her my raincoat and we rushed across the muddy parking lot to the wooden porch of the restaurant. Several truck drivers were drinking beer at the stainless steel bar and a Viennese businessman was treating his secretary to a late lunch. He was aged 60, she was nineteen, I filed away mentally. We settled down into a cubicle swarthed in fish-nets, which had been the owner's idea of an original decor, but it was perfect for the extra privacy and concealment which it provided.

The menu was embarrassingly devoid of imagination. Steaks, schnitzels and gulasch. In a would-be Viennese Danube fish restaurant there were no fish. Except those imported frozen from Japan. I ordered the best white wine they could present, sent the bottle back when it appeared luke warm, received another bottle in a bucket filled with melted ice, and poured a glass for Daria.

'I think you are an infiltrator,' Daria said, raising her glass in my direction. 'A man of impersonation.'

'Impersonating and infiltrating exactly what?'

'Infiltrating the Vienna embassy of the Union of Soviet Socialist Republics. When you speak any language other than Russian you don't talk like a Russian. You make several errors of taste, but your dress is superior to that of your colleagues and their bag suits. And as far as I can judge, you do not think with the typical bureaucratic anxiety of a Soviet official.'

She was lovely as she said this, despite the fact that she unjustly criticised my taste. I sank into the gaze of her oval eyes.

'There is no reason why we Russians cannot combine the advantages and achievements of our system with certain manners thought to be pleasant and acceptable in the West. And, don't forget. I have served abroad for most of my diplomatic career. I have been away from the typical bureaucratic mentality.'

'No *Russki* can ever escape from it, silly. But at least you have suppressed it. You seem to reason like a normal citizen who is not constantly paranoid about his police dossier.'

She reached across the table and clasped both my hands with her long, tapered fingers.

'And that makes you a man, Sergei. I cannot tolerate being with a person terrified of informers snapping his photograph.'

If that was her definition of bravery, in my fear of photographs and of discovery I was certainly less courageous than I was leading her to believe. But don't elaborate, don't elaborate, I told myself very quickly.

I asked her about the studies she had followed, and she told me about her courses in Sofia and Munich and Vienna and the films which she had assisted to edit. She talked effortlessly about the classics of Soviet cinema and we argued whether Eisenstein could have been successful had he utilised colour. I said Potemkin and Alexander Nevskii were unthinkable in colour. But she wasn't so certain, Antonioni had done it hadn't he, switched from neo-realism to colour in *Il Desserto Rosso*. I said this contention was preposterous. Don't start switching from Eisenstein to some effete latin Italian. She said watch who you're calling effete, any man who had a mistress like Monica Vitti was a pretty virile *byk*.

With several bottles of wine and the hours we talked there and the wonderful blurred vision of Daria's face close to mine. . . Olga. Olga and I never discussed anything. Olga. We never talked together, not even of her endless studies of Soviet models of advanced macroeconomics. The short clipped hair. Touching the nape of the neck.

'*Zahlen*!' I suddenly yelled for the waiter.

Rain hammered against the window panes.

'But Sergei, I wish to finish my—'

I flung schilling notes down upon the table, scooped her up under my raincoat, and dashed through the rain to the car.

We bundled into the front seat and slammed the doors. We were soaked. Her linen shirt was drenched with rain and clung to her lithe body.

We stared wildly at one another. I could see she was wearing a loose fitting, flesh-tinted brassière. I touched it.

'Sergei, please.'

'Daria darling.'

'Darling not in the automobile.'

I removed the limp shirt and was kissing her breasts.

'Sweetest it's not a cattle stampede,' she gasped, lifting my head and kissing me on the mouth.

CraaaK.

A tree branch had ripped loose in the wind. What if

it crashed across the car body?

'Yes you can do that again.'

How could I explain that at the embassy garage? If the tree crashed on us?

'Daria dearest.'

'Watch the Nikon – the camera.'

We had wrenched around and crawled onto the back seat.

'The Nikon.'

Her wet black hair streamed across my face. I bit her brown shoulder, struggled with the brassière strap with its little label, which said 'Boutiques Nina Ricci Faubourg St Honoré'.

'Ah. Please.'

'Daria, beautiful.'

'That is very pleasant.'

'Yes. *Da. Da.*'

'Umm. Wow.'

Parisian underwear.

'Yes keep doing that sweetheart.'

'You like that.'

'That is very beautiful. Umm.'

My muscles jerked rigid with tension. Pressing against my back was the cold metal barrel of a. . .

'Don't stop!'

The damn thing was digging into my back. What was I pressing against?

'Yee, you put me on fire and you cease.'

'Daria. . .' what the hell was I lying on?

'Make up your mind!' she hissed. 'Damn it, you've got me half way across the fence!'

Click. Some piece of metal machinery clicked beneath me. I rolled over, rubbing my back.

'Thanks a lot, wonderful lesson in unfulfilled flaming passions,' she said archly as she sat up, clipped her brassière and pulled on her shirt.

'You've been rolling around on my expensive camera sweetest. Be more prudent with your next little *cinq à sept.*' She drew a deep breath, threw back her head, ran a hand through her wet hair and climbed back over to the front seat.

Wearily I dragged myself out in the rain, opened the front door and settled behind the steering wheel. I switched the starter. The motor hacked and sputtered. I thought with panic, what would I do if the damn thing didn't start? Call the tow truck? The Austrian automobile society? It could be a complete disaster. What would they report? What was a drenched Soviet diplomat doing with a half-nude Bulgarian girl in the rain by the Danube?

'Damn!'

Daria had pulled down the visor mirror and was combing her hair.

'It doesn't work.'

She glared at me in silence.

'The engine is not going to start!'

'Don't pump the accelerator. Calm down.'

Splutter and cough.

'*Gavno*!'

'Be patient.'

Finally, on the verge of despair, blue smoke burped out of the exhaust pipe. The motor jerked to life. Slowly I drove back through the wet streets towards Vienna.

'I want to get out by the underground metro at Karlsplatz.'

'Very well.'

I pulled through the sodden traffic and stopped by the broken curbing left unrepaired for the past six months.

'Don't run away from me!' I whispered feverishly.

'I'll run from bloody whom I please!' she hissed.

'Who do you think you own!'

Desperately I grasped her by the wrist. I could not let her leave me like this.

'Kiss me, Daria!'

'I will kiss you, Sergei,' leaning towards me, smiling. 'And shall I photograph it for your papas, uncles and wives?'

She slammed the door and ran away in the rain.

It is unclear how many minutes I sat there slumped exhausted over the steering wheel. Finally an Opel taxi pulled behind me and began flashing his lights for the parking space. I jammed the Lada into gear and drove slowly to the 19th District.

'Typical Vienna summer,' said Olga as I shuffled through the door. 'You are wet like a poodle.'

'Yes, it is quite damp really.'

The living room was filled with packing boxes.

'Suitcases?'

'Of course, suitcases. You forget I have examinations to conclude. The schedule was telexed to the embassy this afternoon.'

'Which flight?' I felt wrung out and emaciated, like pasta shredded through a noodle machine.

'The direct Moscow flight tomorrow. Is that agreeable for you?'

'Yes. Yes. Of course. It is acceptable.'

'Papa was in the Western press again today. About the petroleum exchanges and concessions to the British.'

'You must ask him if it is all beneficial.'

'I have telexed Mama to meet me with Anatoli at the airport.'

'Tell him I want to know how his English progresses.'

'I shall.'

I studied Olga's neatly combed, short blonde hair.

As she rustled with the packing boxes her strong bosom was rigidly controlled by Soviet underwear.

Chapter 7

'*Tochno*. Sit down,' said Chervenkov.

I took a seat in a metal-backed chair obviously designed by the Romanov Inquisition. But I did not give way to an attack of nerves. This summons to the KGB *Rezident*'s embassy office was undoubtedly routine.

'I realise that you were given independence. To determine this, this operation against the man Westfall.' Chervenkov chipped out his sentences like a chisel striking sheet steel. 'But three weeks have passed. You have done nothing.' He leaned forward in the leather swivel chair and ran his hand through his heavy black hair.

The office was windowless. In addition to a glowering portrait of our President, Ministry of Interior photographs hung on the walls depicting Soviet birch forests and arctic lakes. A plastic-bladed East German desk fan lapped at the stale air. I smoothed the creases in my suit and remembered how this Service always pushed you, gave you extended parametres and then cut the time limits in half. Or offered year-long deadlines, then demanded impossible results in six months.

'For your knowledge,' Chervenkov continued with mock politeness, 'while you sit here spinning out elaborate theories the Americans have just approached another Soviet official. Financial inducements were made to a communications clerk in our Milan consulate. I am pleased to record that the offer was rejected, undoubtedly with indignation,' he stated with sarcasm.

Chervenkov was too professional to push my pace, I reasoned quickly. But he clearly faced growing dissatisfaction and pressure from his own superiors.

'So, any bright comments?' he growled.

'The American agents obviously intensify a planned, coordinated campaign against us. But that should not be allowed to affect the methodology employed in this embassy.'

'Methodology be damned! Tactics be damned! I need results!'

'Results are precisely what I intend to produce. Within the correct time sequence.' It was the age-old story, I reasoned. Flaccid bureaucrats somewhere up in the system had panicked and were demanding an instant and successful completion to a high-risk field operation.

Scowling, Chervenkov posed some technical questions about our monitoring operation which I answered effortlessly. Yes, I replied, it was correct that Westfall's telephone calls were totally routine. Chervenkov asked me about the man-hours required to monitor, translate and type the transcripts when I began thinking about Olga. Over two weeks. No letters. No cable messages to the embassy.

Listening to the dull beat of the plastic fan I heard once again the roar of the Aeroflot passenger aircraft lurching down the asphalt of the Vienna runway. Then quiet. The empty apartment, with water dripping at night from a faulty attachment.

Chervenkov was growling, 'What of Westfall's pretences of employment?'

'He goes through the efforts and motions, as they say. Departs for his 19th District office in the late mornings. Eats supper in a *gasthaus*. Sausages, when he isn't cooking spaghetti for his Yugoslav girl friend in the flat.'

'Too goddam clever. He's laying too quiet. Did he detect your team, Sergei? I'll have you and your people doing inventories on typewriter ribbons in Vladivostok!'

'Twice a week they hit each other and knock themselves down.'

'What are you talking about! Are you distorting all this?'

'Westfall and some Scotsmen have started rugby training. In a flat land with mosquitoes across the Danube. I am distorting nothing whatsoever.'

During the past fourteen days, I recalled, I had left exactly seven messages for Daria Kaladzhiev with the portier at the university. I had proposed an evening concert at Schönbrunn. I suggested a boating excursion to Krems on the Danube. Why did she not reply? Why was she allowing the weeks to drain past? Would I continue to live in Vienna and not be allowed to communicate? Could I not telephone her at the Bulgarian embassy?

'You are giving this assignment against Westfall and the I Board your full attention?' Chervenkov was asking.

By God, I was a man in my thirties and reduced to leaving folded envelopes with doorkeepers! But of course! That was too formal and romantic and polite for the lady! She was out at this moment smoking noxious drugs. Running around with the photograph crowd. Attending pretentious – what do you call them – *vernissages*?

'It is my complete preoccupation,' I replied smoothly. 'My other assignments have been cancelled.'

'Not much return for the effort, that what it looks like to you?' he clicked his beaver-like chisel teeth.

'Any American capitalist would pull out his money.'

'I have contacted the frontier police of adjacent socialist states.'

'And what is that supposed to mean? I thought you said Westfall wasn't moving.'

'He left Vienna once in the last ten days – for thirty-six hours. If he has built a cover as an East–West business specialist then he must have established a travel pattern. I refuse to be rushed before we establish that pattern.'

'That method sounds like gypsies over in Hungary reading tea leaves. An admirable means of forecasting. Very scientific . . .'

Olga had passed through the airport customs with three suitcases packed with duty-free gifts for her parents. I had purchased Adidas running shoes for Anatoli.

She had been very placid. It was though I had been saying goodbye to a business colleague and not my wife.

'Is there any greeting for Papa?'

'Tell him I don't understand this petroleum concession business.'

'Perhaps it is a state secret.'

'How can it be a state secret if it's discussed in the Western press?'

I watched her queue with the other Soviet wives. Tall, strong, with narrow face and cold grey eyes, standing a head taller than the sausage squat Political Counsellor's wife, erect and distinguished among the other Russian diplomatic ladies who were little more dignified than a pack of fishmongers. She had pursed her fine lips toward me in a dry kiss, entered passport control and never looked back . . .

'. . . You better sort the wheat from the oats and tell me what you're planning to do,' snapped my *Rezi-*

dent, Chervenkov. 'This caution stuff they teach young intelligence officers in their diapers has its limits.'

'Naturally, caution has disadvantages. But at this moment Westfall is presenting no target whatsoever.'

'Well, the sonofabitch! You were the bright young man, may I remind you, who suggested he *was* a target! You made the protracted speech about our Russian rationality, methodology, and resistance to impulse.'

'Westfall's unimaginative, spartan existence in Vienna is clearly a front,' I shot back, determined not to be intimidated. 'I want to see the record. Where he's been moving in Eastern Europe. Under what pretences. Then we can start moving in . . .'

Angrily, Chervenkov slapped the papers on his desk and I asked myself how I could have handled it more competently. Should I simply have driven to the Bulgarian embassy and asked Ambassador Kaladzhiev to deliver my little Pushkinite love notes to his high-breasted daughter? Daria's breasts, I slipped into memory of my first kisses in the automobile in the rain, deeply tanned and oval, rising to the point of her dark nipples, thrusting against her Parisian brassière, was another man touching the point of those breasts, was she now with another lover? Would she allow her breasts to be fondled by an Austrian? No, it was impossible! My stomach caught at the revulsion of the picture. Would-be Austrian lovers, miserable scum, their swing bellies fat as swine at the trough, but if she allowed a Frenchman . . . she had been wearing French underwear, was that why she would not return my messages? Was Daria allowing herself to be the mistress of some spineless, back-haired skinny Frenchman in expensive sun glasses? Sweat erupted from my temples. I grasped a handkerchief and mopped my face in the stale heat. I would not permit her to be handled and fondled by such riffraff, hooligans . . .

'Moving in? Moving in!' Chervenkov rasped. 'By all appearances you are hanging back in the shadows trembling with fright. Westfall first contacted you, are you keeping a hold on the bastard?'

'He telephoned me to play this brutal tackling game, this rugby with them, across the Danube.'

'Well, you're the athlete of the embassy! Go out and knock the hell out of him! Latch onto him like a blood sucking leech. Drain out every drop of information. His girls and his money and his bank account and his boss. Understood?'

'All very clear,' I stood up in a hurry, wiping my face. *Faubourg St Honoré, the brassière label had read. Nina Ricci.*

'Now get the hell out of here. Get some results.'

'*Do svidaniya.*'

'*Do svidaniya.*'

I gave a stiff official nod of the head and took my exit. I seethed. Chervenkov knew this rowdy stampede, this demand for precipitate action, contradicted his own conservative principles. Fortunately, I was indeed confident that a study of Westfall's movements would fill in some of the dark holes in our intelligence.

I walked briskly down the linoleum carpet which runs the length of the embassy's fifth floor. This section was sealed from other functional departments and controlled entirely by the KGB apparatus. In addition to Chervenkov's austere office and the sound-proof conference chamber, housed on this floor was a code and scrambled UHF communications section; a locked depository of weapons, penetration devices and electronic scanning equipment; our special finance and 'black' banking transfer unit; and the registry section with its Honeywell computer we had purchased from the Americans, the device used to check Daria Kaladzhieva upon my earlier telephone enquiry.

Syzmanski and the technicians lived up here most of their working lives; somehow Razin had secured a tiny office near the communications section. Other embassy officials with various titles on their calling cards had locked offices in this section. It is not germane to discuss here their identities.

Chervenkov had granted me a coveted corner office with soundproof windows, although my official telephone listing was with the third-floor economics section. All of the offices and installations had southern exposure. We had no interest in facing the West German embassy and their listening devices across Reisnerstrasse on the northern side of the building.

I checked with the communications room to see if a cable had arrived from Olga. No cable. Nothing. No communication. Why? Was she isolating me in loneliness? In cold. Frost. Which of my actions had driven her to silence? I slouched down the corridor toward my office, lonely and confused over the total silence from my wife and her entanglements in doctoral thesis and examinations.

'Syzmanski!' I spoke quietly into my telephone receiver.

'Sir!'

'Bring the telexed replies concerning Westfall's travel into other socialist countries.'

'It is not complete.'

'What do you mean not complete?'

'The Romanians never answered our cable.'

The sons of bitching Romanians. I cradled my head in my hands. A pack of gypsies. They should be expelled from the Warsaw Pact. We should insist that the Romanians be incorporated into the Western NATO alliance, to spread confusion and dissent there. I whispered that Syzmanski should fetch whatever material the other socialist brothers had been kind enough to produce.

Waiting for the fat Syzmanski to waddle down the corridor I telephoned registry for information about oil concessions to the British.

'What concessions would those be?' said the dull clerk over the telephone line. What was becoming of our staff efficiency?

'Ask the Honeywell device we pay you hard currency to operate, fool. It is throughout the *Financial Times*. Apparently we give something away to British Petroleum.'

By this time Syzmanski had shuffled through the door, and despite the humidity, was still wearing his tiny loden hat.

'It's sort of like my grandmother from Grodno,' said the White Russian who, as usual, reeked of sardines.

I grasped the thick file of telex reports from Budapest, Prague, Warsaw and Berlin. The Russian grammar was appalling. Although we had security advisers sitting in every intelligence apparat in Eastern Europe, the local bastards still could not write proper Russian.

'And why, may I ask, like your grandmother from Grodno?'

'She never crossed the frontier to Poland but at the same place,' said Syzmanski. 'We later learned she was having a liaison once a month, with a Polish colonel. She was aged sixty-six.'

After half an hour's study I began to see what he was talking about. Of fourteen frontier-crossings out of Austria into the socialist countries during the past year, this man Westfall had made twelve of them at a border station called Mikulov. To our accommodating, neighbourly, Socialist Republic of Czechoslovakia.

Chapter 8

'Mikulov.'

'It's north of Vienna on the—'

'Thank you, Syzmanski. I am perfectly aware that Mikulov is the CSSR frontier crossing on the highway from Vienna to Brno. And that it's fully decorated with all the barbed wire and spotlights which the capitalist press seem to love so much. What else do the Czechs have to tell us?'

'Nothing. All we asked was Westfall's border crossings.'

Sometime, some day, I would appreciate the development of some independent initiative among the allied intelligence services. With minimal effort the Czechs could have given me Westfall's itinerary within their country. Do I have to fly to Prague and sack their chief of liaison?

I flung Syzmanski a stenographer's pad.

'Take these notes. Today is Friday, but by Monday at 12 noon the Czechs will meet me in Brno. District office of security for Moravia. With: (a) photocopies of Westfall's visa applications . . . .'

'*Mozhno, pomedlennyeye* . . .' He was asking me to slow down.

'. . . (b) Copies of hotel registrations for nights Westfall resided within the CSSR. (c) Commentaries.'

'Commentaries?'

'Usual paraphernalia. Informers' dispositions. Was Westfall seen in public restaurants, cinemas. Follow-up debriefing of his business contacts, if any. Girls if any. Usual militia reports, speeding, traffic fines.'

Syzmanski scribbled desperately to keep up with my dictation. I yanked the phone from the receiver and requested the operator to connect me with Westfall at his business address, the fictitious leasing East–West business office in the 19th District.

'The poor Czechs will have to work through the weekend to obtain your documents,' lamented Syzmanski, rubbing his fat hand across his lips.

'One is touched with your concern. (d) Exits. Did Westfall exit same crossing point as entrance? (e) Entrance from adjoining socialist countries.'

'Uh, I don't understand.'

'We know he has visited Eastern Europe on fourteen occasions, twelve of which have been recorded to the CSSR. Has he by any chance re-entered the CSSR on two occasions via Hungary or Poland?'

The telephone purred.

'Well now Sergei, hi there!'

'And how is Vienna's leading East–West trader?'

'Reasonably prosperous, but it's an art,' laughed Westfall. 'How about it?'

'You're referring to this, this rugby practice?' with a wink at Syzmanski.

'Never too old. Got to start sometime. We have a squad scrimmage Saturday at eleven.'

'Eleven? What about six in the evening, it will be very very hot.'

'A lot hotter than you think. We'll see how tough the violent Russkies are.'

One would indeed see. I told him I'd be there, thus conforming with Chervenkov the *Rezident's* directives.

'Transportation,' I continued dictating to Syzmanski. 'I drive my Lada. But coordinate with Mikulov frontier police so that I do not have to wait in a queue for passport and customs control.'

'You will be sort of conspicuous,' Syzmanski said, reasonably. 'If you drive a private Lada past that two kilometre line of cars waiting up there.'

'Very well. Requisition one of the embassy's black Volgas with CD plates. As long as I'm an official with a big car, the Austrians waiting in queues will be too cowardly to complain.'

As Syzmanski rose the clerk from registry knocked at the door. He carried a folder of press statements and computer sheets relating to Soviet ministerial transactions with British Petroleum.

I poured over the material for the next hour. Dipl. Ing. G. V. Sokolovskiy, Soviet Minister for Petroleum and Mining – my father-in-law – had granted a multi-million pound sterling contract to Constructors John Brown and British Petroleum for technology, platforms and rig equipment to assist in offshore petroleum exploration. Geographical areas included the Sea of Azov, Sea of Okhotsk in the Soviet Far East, and the Kara and Barents Seas in the Arctic.

British technology was selected in the face of rigorous American competition due to their experience gained in North Sea oil exploration. Olga's father was quoted as saying, 'Our technology is founded on rig drilling to a maximum depth of 100 metres of sea water. The British experience provides assistance to roughly double this depth.'

To offset partially the hard currency outlays to the UK contracting team, the file continued, the Soviet Union agreed for an unrevealed period to provide British Petroleum with 10 million tons of crude petroleum annually at prices set seven per cent below the prevailing OPEC levels.

The contractual terms were described as 'discriminatory' and 'technologically questionable' by the unsuccessful consortium of American bidders, which included Gulf Oil and Standard Oil of California.

Looking back, this information should have been highly significant, the key to many puzzles. But at the moment it told me nothing, nothing at all.

I snapped shut the dossier, which I returned to the registry. Sniff. Somewhere in the corridors Razin was lurking. I could sniff his perfume.

One more minor task awaited me. I tapped out the digital code for the electric lock which gave access to the banking section and entered the financial office for a little monthly transaction. This involved currency transfer from a Viennese bank (which I do not choose to mention here) to a special numbered account in Klagenfurt, in the southern province of Carinthia along the Yugoslav border.

The Americans, I believe, term this 'laundering'. I'm not concerned with what it's called. The Austrian no-names-asked confidential *Losungwort* banking system is a wonderful mechanism for moving anonymous amounts of money around the country. By contrast the much-vaunted Swiss banking secrecy is about as discreet as a World Cup final.

The clerk pushed the buff-coloured authorisation documents across the counter for my signature. Certain gentlemen of my acquaintance in the south could now be assured of their next monthly stipend valued at 30,000 Austrian schillings.

'Doon rrn akrs the pitch man, yu must ead dirrekt too th gool!' a big, blond Scotsman was bellowing.

Thump.

The oval rugby ball hung lazily in the air. I wiped

sweat from my eyes.

'Call for it, Sergei.'

I took it as I had learned in soccer in my gymnasium days, that is to say, cradling the ball with both arms to my chest. It was then I was tackled somewhat simultaneously by six of the opposition. The ball squirted loose upon impact, some Austrian stamped cleat marks on the small of my back, and I lay sucking fish-like and frantically for breath as Westfall pounced on the loose ball and turned back toward goal before he was crashed out of bounds.

'Time,' the referee sounded his whistle.

Blood trickled from a cut lip and someone had poked a thumb in my left eye. Both knees were burned raw from the dirt pitch. Heat shimmered off the Danube which flowed dirty grey past the playing fields. The Viennese sun, notable for its absence most of this summer, glared down with all the mercy of a vulture pecking carrion in the desert.

And that was the first half.

Westfall, who had been spiked in the shin, threw me a lemon half.

'He-el, that thing hurts! Can you make it without packing up?'

I dragged myself up from the pitch. Someone handed me a pail of water which I doused over my head. I winced as the acid of the lemon rind washed through my cut mouth.

'I can make it without packing up if you start explaining the rules.'

'The rule book is about two hundred pages thick.'

'What did I do wrong back there taking the ball?'

'Not a thing. Next time holler "mark".'

'"Mark"?'

'It's like a fair catch.'

'Listen to me Wes. Explain these fine points logically when survival is in question. Don't confuse me with your *Amerikanskii* football jargon.'

'Sorry. Holler "mark" and they can't knock you down.' He pronounced 'can't' '*kaint*'. 'But after a mark, you can't run with the ball.'

Westfall's thick dark hair and British-model moustache were matted with sweat and dust. The scar on his cheek stood out grey against his sunburn. In shorts, jersey and rugger socks he wasn't barrel-chested like the Austrian players on the team, but tall and lanky, muscles taut and stomach as firm as sheet-iron.

The other players were a wild assembly of Scots, Welsh, an Irish doctor, a massive New Zealander, five or six American students obviously acquainted with their own football but struggling with the complex rugby rules, and three Austrians. It was one of these latter who had planted his boot in my back. Werner, he said his name was.

Werner with his massive biceps and blond hair sauntered over, whacked me on the back and bawled out that maybe I should revert to playing chess like all Russians, no? Maybe that was less dangerous, more appropriate and mental?

'Shall we start?' the English referee said primly.

That second half dissolved into a dusty, thirsty blur of scrummage. Westfall explained that our side's tactic was to batter the opposition with our eight forwards, among whom I was included. Beat them in the pack, he told me, and it sounded positive but this entailed furious shoving and kicking in a wild mêlée.

Near the end of the half our pack drove the opposing forwards off the ball, which was scooped up on the run by our scrum-half. He plunged across for a try which put us in the lead for the first time in the afternoon.

The other side had only one more chance to equalise, and this was when Werner handled a loose ball, flattened one of our backs with a stiffarm and bulled for the goal. One metre out I slammed my shoulder deep under his ribs and he coughed up the ball.

Assisted by another player the Austrian limped quietly off the pitch.

We showered under frigid water in steel drums and then the parched players descended on a shaded beer garden.

'And this is your idea of how to spend a Saturday morning?' I asked Westfall, draining in my thirst a *krügel* glass of beer and yelling at the waitress for more.

'Twice a week,' he laughed, slapping his empty glass on a beer mat. 'We take on Lokomotiva of Brno pretty soon.'

'Brno is in Czechoslovakia?' I inserted quickly, the intelligence professional not yet completely dulled by the rigours of rugby training. 'Why play in Czechoslovakia?'

'No one else in Austria will organise a rugby club, so we've got to play against other teams outside. Listen Sergei, I have been wanting to ask you, uh, what can you tell me about Lermontov?'

Behind us, across a green table stacked with beer mugs, the Scots had launched into their repertoire of rugger songs.

> Four and twenty virgins
> Came down from Inverness. . .

Or, something similar, if I understood correctly their Gaelic brogue.

'Lermontov? The last time I read Lermontov was sixteen years ago when I was trying to impress a girl literature student from Kiev.' This was more or less true, but again Westfall's capacity of bounding to the unexpected kept me scrambling mentally to catch up.

'"Taman is the foulest pest hole on all of the Black Sea coast."' He drained another beer glass. 'Know what that's from?'

> . . . An' when they went a' home again
> They were four-an-twenty less. . .

'It's one of those Black Sea stories. Where the hero is an officer serving in the infantry against the wild mountain rebels.'

> . . . Come on Dinah show us your leg
> Show us your leg. . .

'Ever heard of a story by Chekhov on the Black Sea called 'The Duel'? In that one short story there is every major element of classic Russian literature. The superfluous man. Cold, nineteenth-century science versus the human heart. The warm south against the corrupt, frozen society of the north. . .'

He went on and on, really excited. And Westfall, I could have added, 'The Duel' is excellently suited to modern adaptation, provided one has the talent. He didn't know it, but I had photocopies of his hackneyed and incomplete attempt in our registry files.

'Now see here,' he-ah, he lapsed into his provincial American drawl, 'what is there to keep somebody from writing that story in modern times?'

> Come on Dinah show us your leg
> A yard above the knee.

'Why nothing at all!' I beamed enthusiastically. I had recovered my breath and quenched my thirst. 'I would encourage it. It would be a significant contribution.'

He asked me about some of Pushkin's stories which

I recalled only dimly. After all, my primary, ostensible field was economics. Then with the increasingly ribald Scots chorus in the background the conversation turned around to girls. And Westfall solicited my opinion on Austrian girls, and what Russian girls were like.

Looking at him, the tousled hair, Lacoste jersey and Levi jeans, sandals, his long frame slouched over two chairs, I reminded myself that he was a professional American operative with at least one murder to his record. *Treat him as a dangerous species of reptile*, I tried to shake myself out of my post-rugby stupor.

'How's Olga?' he drawled. He had met her once long ago at some official reception.

'Quite well and healthy, thank you.'

'Thesis coming along OK?' I believe I had told Westfall once that she was working on her dissertation. *But verify the report in registry of that previous conversation.*

The other players had begun to gather their kitbags, and the New Zealander made a point of crossing the garden to tell me to keep working at it. I could be of assistance in the line-outs and rucks, he told me, although I by no means understood his rugby terminology.

Westfall lifted his kit and asked if I needed transportation, which I declined, nodding towards my parked Lada.

'Olga's speciality is, ah, Soviet planning models?' he pressed, standing up from the table.

'Something of the kind,' I laughed. Why was it that he was continually forcing me into hastily conceived laughter to hide a potential embarrassment? Was he going to ask me if she was now in Moscow? Should I conceal her return home? 'Although I am certain she could write that short story for you, if she chose.'

'Give her my best wishes and recommendations,' he smiled and loped away, leaving me to walk stiffly to my car thinking of a lot of things but questioning primarily Westfall's sudden-found interest in Olga.

Weary in frame and depressed in spirit I limped into the hallway of my residence in the 19th District. Though it was Saturday, I opened the mailbox on the slight chance that Olga would have mailed a letter by express post.

A postcard tumbled out and floated to the concrete floor.

I retrieved it hurriedly. Had Olga . . . finally. . . No. A Vienna postmark. A postcard with a photograph of the swimming pool in the 19th District above Grinzing. Who? No message. Stamp. And handwritten date. The date was today, I noticed excitedly. Mailed yesterday, post-dated today, a swimming. . . Daria was at the pool in Grinzing. Now. Was she there now? It was four in the afternoon. Too late? Had I been a fool to linger after the rugby? I rushed into my apartment, seized my swimming things, dashed to the Lada and drove frantically through the twisting streets of Grinzing and ground gears up the foothills of the Vienna woods to this most elite of Vienna's public pools.

There was the usual administration with the cashier, then I changed hurriedly into my blue trunks and strode out onto the grassy esplanade surrounding the large pool. Hundreds of the more refined classes of Viennese girls and young men lounged around on beach chairs. Where was she? Was she here at all? Would she be wearing a string bikini costume? Would she be revealing the trace of her breasts and loins under the most sheer of material? Were there fat, obnoxious Austrians leering around her? Or was it farce, had she trapped me, later to jeer at my gullibility?

I had begun to spread my beach towel on the lawn when through the crowd of Austrians I saw her walking toward me. She had just come from the pool and the water rippled from her wet hair down her glistening tanned shoulders. To my surprise Daria was not in a risqué bikini, but I don't want to give the impression it was all ruffles, skirts and bloomers. She wore a single piece, white bathing costume trimmed up from her thighs almost to her waist, accentuating the marvellous curve of those coltish brown thighs. The bodice had been opened and held across her breasts by a single link of golden thread.

'Ciao! Hey, know something?!'

I shook my head, throat knotted, reached out for her brown arm and pulled her down beside me.

'You're pretty good! A lot of guys wouldn't get the point of that postcard!'

Heads turned as Daria walked past, and quite a few more swerved in our direction as she began speaking English. The hell with it. This was the last place I would encounter Razin and his snooping minions.

'Look Daria, I almost didn't get the point. Next time you decide to communicate leave less to chance.'

'But you're glad you're here?'

'Delighted. The view is magnificent.'

'Not scared of your embassy keepers? No one from Soviet protocol in attendance?' she laughed. 'And where, may I ask, is Madame Olga?'

'My wife is in Moscow completing her examinations.'

'Aa ha, for long?' but some of the teasing pitch

went out of her laughter.

'It appears for very long. I am completely uninformed regarding her future intentions.'

We chatted on like this, but I realised she was much more tense than I had previously experienced. We swam together. Lay beside one another on the grass and talked, but neither of us mentioned the horrible afternoon by the Danube in the rain. Then the heat of the day passed, and as the air cooled Daria suggested we leave.

I waited for her outside the changing rooms and we walked together towards my Lada.

'How about letting me have the keys, no?'

What was happening? What had changed with the once-remote Daria?

'Be my guest.'

'Just how far does that invitation extend?'

'As far as you wish to accept it.'

My throat was as dry as steel filings when I said that, and it got a lot drier as she drove in the direction of my residence. Now, from such a distant omniscient perspective, I know that was the last moment I could have intervened to halt a process whose evolution, even then, was fast slipping beyond my control. Ah yes, so many technical instruments were open to me. Switch off the ignition. Invent a sudden recall to the embassy. Or say no, no.

'Yes, Sergei?'

'Yes,' I said.

Without a lot of complications we began shedding clothes as soon as we entered the flat and amid now unrestrained kisses went straight to bed.

'Why is it,' Daria asked me much later, 'you are permitted to live in a private residence? Most of the other Russian diplomats have to stay in a housing compound.'

Daria was sitting cross-legged on the bed beside me, sharing a bottle of Crimean champagne I had found in the refrigerator.

'Why are you, the daughter of a Warsaw Pact country ambassador, permitted to study in the capitalist West?'

'Because Daddy has what is known as old-fashioned influence.'

'He pulled strings.'

'He pulled so many wires it looked at one stage like he was directing a puppet show.'

'I am here by virtue of my own talent,' I laughed, lazily holding out my glass to be filled.

'It's impossible. I understand Olga's father is a big-shot,' she replied, using the American terminology.

'That has nothing to do with my permission to live in a private flat. Put bluntly, they trust me.'

'Do they, uh, er . . . you know? She waved the champagne bottle around, pointing at the ceiling to indicate listening devices.

'Little hypocrite!' I rolled over and whacked her bare bottom. 'And you portray me as terrified of Soviet security!'

'Well, you're right, but, ah, do they do sound recording?'

'How should I know? I am an official in very good standing. Why worry?'

'I mean,' she smiled coquettishly, 'this is the age of microphones and beep-beep machinery and bouncing waves off windows and laser beams. Theoretically nothing is private.'

'Some events, dear Daria,' I said, putting down the champagne glass, taking her by the shoulders, and kissing her softly on the lips, 'some events I intend to keep very private.'

It was in the evening when I woke up to hear her taking a shower. She came out lithe and sparkling without a great deal of clothes on and proceeded to rummage around the apartment, opening drawers, pulling out Olga's dresses and looking at my suits.

I can assure you, it's an experience to have a gorgeous twenty-three-year-old Bulgarian girl walking around your house with nothing on but a pair of bikini underpants inspecting closets and commenting on your wardrobe.

'Maybe your wife should start her own sewing,' Daria mewed. 'These Soviet dresses of dear Olga are museum relics. And your Austrian suits are from department stores? You had me fooled, Sergei.' She stood there, wagging a finger in my direction, the tip of her beautiful tongue clicking off my sartorial shortcomings.

'*Bitte, der Herr. Womit kann ich Ihnen behilflich sein*?' queried the tall, aloof chief fitter of Heinz Mohr, tailor to the Viennese Establishment at 8:30 on Monday morning.

'I am from an embassy. I wish to be measured for several new suits of clothes.'

'Indeed yes, sir,' he remarked coolly, glancing at my dark-blue business suit. 'One would understand why, sir.'

Chapter 9

The Austrian frontier guards saw the CD plates and waved me towards what the capitalist press refers to as no-mans-land, The Iron Curtain. Rubbish. A few tank traps here and there, triple aprons of barbed wire, ploughed strips, spotlight towers and minefields, but that was the prerogative of the Czechs. If they so chose to regulate their frontier what right has the Western press to complain? No heroin shipments, pornographic literature, dope, drugs and hippies get through that border, I assure you, in contrast to the porous Austrian frontiers. If *The New York Times*, *Le Monde* and the London *Economist* worried more about their own degenerate societies and grumbled less about the administrative measures of socialist countries. . . .

The road ran downward to a small stream which marked the actual state boundary, then began climbing past fields of ripening grain toward the Czech passport control point. The morning sunlight reflected on the dull yellow baroque towers of the Mikulov cathedral. A cuckoo sang in the forest. That was all very bucolic, but the road was clogged with a queue of one thousand automobiles. I ask you, if our Warsaw Pact nations are such dungeons of terror, as is implied ad nauseam in the *Washington Post*, why in hell are so many Western tourists lining up to enter?

I pulled over into the passing lane and drove toward the first pillbox. A Czech soldier in woollen brown uniform with a green band around his service cap began to unlimber his AK47 assault rifle. Then he noticed my plates, grasped a field telephone, finally nodded and swung back the steel boom which restrained the remaining automobiles.

My passport was stamped at the control station while some German was arguing about obligatory conversion of his Deutschmarks into Czech koruna. In the parking zone two ministry of interior functionaries with mirrors and flashlights were crawling underneath an American Express pullman bus. Large American ladies in floral trousers photographed the deed with their Instamatic cameras.

I reached the Brno suburbs by 11:30, but the traffic crawled to a halt behind a work crew ripping up tram tracks. Across a field of brown weeds smoke belched from a metal foundry. Dust hung in the air, coating the broken cobblestones and rusted fencing of a scrap metal lot. High on a hill line a Habsburg fortress peered glumly on the mediaeval sections of the city.

The repairs would delay my arrival past 12:00, and this was intolerable. I jerked around the stalled line of trucks and buses, flicked my headlights violently enough to capture the attention of a bored policeman who sprang to life and waved me past the construction site. Threading through the narrow streets in the centre of Brno I walked into the security office for Moravia – the Czech midlands – as the chimes struck noon.

Three Czechs were waiting for me with stuffed briefcases. Good sign, I told myself, nodding to the officials but not shaking hands. Perhaps we could settle down to an efficient conduct of affairs.

A stout, uniformed woman police official brought out a plate of cold ham, brown bread, pickles, mustard and Czech slivovica.

Immediately, I raised my eyebrows:

'No beer?'

The policewoman looked at the officials for a proper reply.

'You see, our Pilsner and Budweiser are exported to the West for hard currency,' one powerful chested Czech policeman answered me icily.

'What the hell! Do you have a duty-free, hard-currency shop in all of Brno?'

I'll be damned if I'll journey to Czechoslovakia and not drink good beer. The hell with them. That American Express bus with the plump ladies was probably now parked outside the duty-free shop loading up on Pilsner.

Making no attempt to conceal his displeasure, the heavy Czech official noted that perhaps suitable bottles of beer could be obtained from the tourist hotel and I said that was admirable.

We turned to a discussion of Westfall's travel routes, but it was obvious that I was not among friends. Who portrays the Czechs as supine, cringing and pliable? The three types facing me were as rough as flint. Especially the broad-shouldered policeman with hard blue eyes and a cauliflower ear.

'Tell me something,' I said in Russian as it became obvious they were not particularly enthusiastic about revealing their surveillance methods. 'Is there something in this city called "Lokomotiva Brno"?'

'It's the rugby team.'

'You know that.'

'Of course I know that. I played against them for ten seasons with Spartak Prague,' said the big policeman with the lumped ear.

'Westfall and his Scots are to engage Lokomotiva Brno.'

This was met with raucous laughter.

'Engage who? Engage the reserves, juniors or baby squad? It will be mayhem.'

'It will, will it?' With my cut lip and skinned knees I was impressed by Westfall's colleagues. 'They hit hard.'

'If Lokomotiva Brno does not defeat them we'll mail you a crate of Pilsner,' the big policeman laughed.

As I say, so much for the cliché of the timid Czechs.

Within the past twelve months, the files from the Foreign Ministry's visa office confirmed, Westfall had crossed into the republic on thirteen occasions. Twelve directly from Austria through Mikulov, once via Hungary through Bratislava. Surveillance had been discontinued after the first six crossings.

'Whose idea was that!' I demanded.

'We have had substantial budget problems.'

'*Gavno*! What the hell was his pretext then?'

They insisted it was legitimate. He had served as consultant to a Western engineering corporation involved in modernisation of the Brno 'First Iskra' machine tool plant.

'*Thirteen times*? What was Westfall doing, trying to get himself elected to the trade unions council? It's not good enough,' I emphasised. 'He's been running around your noses and you have no idea of his intentions in Brno. What does "First Iskra" produce, nuclear generating equipment?'

' "First Iskra" makes machine tools,' the blue-eyed cop answered. 'To manufacture diesel engines. Which we must deliver to the Soviet Union. Instead of selling for hard currency on profitable Western markets. Does that answer the question?'

He made his point and the hell with them. They get our Soviet petroleum don't they? 'Show me the reports on his hotel surveillance, before it was so conveniently discontinued.'

They dropped a thin file of Czech-language police

reports on the table, but my concentration disengaged and I saw Daria sitting at Olga's dressing table in the bedroom, combing her long black hair over her naked shoulders . . . the apartment, it could not continue there indefinitely, how often could I induce her to travel beyond Vienna? Had the Bulgarian embassy placed her under surveillance? What about us? Razin? Would he suspect me? Of what? Huh? Of what security violation, tell me that!? What had she said as she left me. We have lost time, Sergei. Women don't say things like that lightly. No longer the mocking Daria. You should not stay away long, she had told me, lying in the half-darkness, tapping the wine glass with her fingernail until it rang crystal before she left me. . .

'Hum?' I asked somewhat fuzzily.

'In other words, to repeat, nothing. Ordinary. Legitimate. Westfall, whatever his real purpose, of which you have not completely informed us, led the life of a model businessman while in Brno.'

'Ende. Fin. The End, is it?' I snapped. 'Nothing more to add?'

'What did you expect us to produce? You Soviets had never informed us that Westfall was to be viewed with suspicion.'

This bickering got us nowhere. I demanded to see the files and for the next thirty minutes struggled through the reports typed in Czech.

'What is this business about the village east of Brno called "Slavkov u Brna"?'

The heavy policeman retrieved the dossier.

'Westfall stated interest in the great Napoleonic battlefield of Austerlitz. It was fought near there. In 1805.'

'I have, after all, read *War and Peace*. What then?'

'Nothing. He would go up there and wander around

the countryside. With books and charts and maps. The police kept him under observation for two or three journeys. Then they, er, dropped it. He appeared to be doing exactly what he said he was doing. Touring Napoleon's battlefield.'

It was so like him, I smiled. Westfall, the amateur short-story writer and rugby player now turned into innocent historian. He had probably spent months reading about Austerlitz to convince these Czechs of his sincerity. My God, it would not have been surprising if he had appeared in tweeds, riding boots and field glasses to complete the charade.

'Now listen carefully,' I said gently in order not to stir further the Czechs' hostility. 'One: register me tonight in your best Brno hotel. Two: contact the local militia chief for this village of Slavkov-Austerlitz. Three: translate for me, no later than tomorrow morning, the complete transcript of the Slavkov field reports *which were judged routine and hence not forwarded to Prague*. Four: at 9:00am tomorrow drive me to Austerlitz and Slavkov. Clear?'

'All very clear,' the Czechs said and not very charmed about it.

Driving towards Slavkov early the next morning we halted first at the Austerlitz battlefield. I am not particularly certain why, but we Europeans do not indulge in the American mania for marking sites of past conflict and slaughter. There was an absence of plaques and fossilised cannon à la Gettysburg or Bull Run.

A light rain had fallen during the evening and the fields of barley and clover were fresh with scent. From the Pratzen Heights I could look across the rolling fields and dimly see Napoleon's position where he waited to launch Marshal Soult and counterattack this centre of the Austrian and Russian armies. That had been a frosty December morning and now the sun was shining but it wouldn't take much effort to visualise the crack of musketry and cannon, billowing smoke and jingle of harness.

The Czech policeman seemed impatient out in the fields under glorious sunshine. They had probably grown up in some urban apartment block so beloved by our socialist planners.

But I was in no hurry. Earlier this morning, looking over the hastily translated police records from Slavkov, Westfall's little game had at last, at last become clear. *Left Austerlitz field and stopped at painter Jan Siska*, read the militia account of his fourth visit to Czechoslovakia which the local authorities had judged as so routine it had not been forwarded in Westfall's master file to Prague. Visit number five: *Austerlitz. Two hours on Pratzen Heights. Siska residence. Return Brno*. After that even the Slavkov militia had stopped reporting, but it was sufficient for my needs.

Regretfully on this wonderfully scented morning I had to continue with my assignment. The Czechs beamed when I told them to drive to Slavkov.

'Militia headquarters?'

'It is no longer necessary. I want to see a man named Siska. Outskirts of Slavkov, address in the files.'

That brought glum glances. They assumed I was using them as tourist guides. I chuckled. Ha. Westfall had brilliantly assessed the Czech mentality. Had he photographed a manufacturing plant at three o'clock in the morning he would have been apprehended within minutes. But walking in the battlefields and calling on a painter?

Shades were hastily pulled down as our black Tatra limousine halted before the Siska house. This was a building of fading bricks on a long street with broken asphalt running off to dust and collectivised grain fields in the distance.

If I had judged correctly Siska would be well past middle age and we could converse in German. I told the policemen to wait in the automobile.

A grey-haired lady opened the door and I was ushered through a hallway to an open courtyard. Obviously, once long ago this had been part of the stables for a large farmhouse, and willow trees swayed in the breeze over the old stone granery. In the midst of the grass sat an old man painting on a tiny patch of canvas pinned to an easel.

'*Grüss Tott, der Herr*,' I said respectfully.

Siska didn't look up.

'*Willkommen, setzen Sie sich*,' he said, staring at his canvas.

His thick shock of hair was iron grey. The fingers holding the wire-thin brush were gnarled with toil. The lady appeared with a carafe of cold white wine. I allowed him to continue with his work.

Siska was a naive painter. I studied the intricate brush strokes and the near-microscopic character of his landscape. The canvas portrayed milk cows flying through the air, storks carrying tiny babies, a barn upended on its corner with grain spilling out, peasants reaping barley, all concentrated in a space less than 10×20 centimetres.

'Ah, my back is pain now, the concentration becomes more difficult. Please.' He poured two glasses of wine.

'I wish to talk of the American, Herr Siska.'

He drank wine and looked at me with steady blue eyes. No reply.

'He purchased at least ten canvases.'

'*Naja*. How can I remember, exactly.'

'For which he paid you, illegally, in American dollars.'

'And you are from the Czech police.'

'No.'

The willow leaves tossed quietly, their white undersides shimmering in the fresh air. I refilled his glass and drank my glass of the cold wine.

'The police. No-one is from the police. Everyone is from the police. I have lived in Slavkov for seventy-five years. Police. I have known Austrian authorities, and Czech gendarmes, and Nazi Gestapo, and now the police with the shiny belts of our new republic. Do not talk to me of not being police.'

'I am from another land, Herr Siska. I would ask you respectfully to believe me when I state that I have authority over even your own police.'

'Now it is another lecture you want?' he chuckled. 'Jan Siska's lecture on believing and trusting?'

'I don't want you to lecture me but I hope you believe me.'

'The wine is good. Here, yes, please drink more. As a special concession,' he laughed, 'the government allows me to keep my own vineyard from which I press this wine.'

The wine was very good.

'Ten canvases?'

'The last time he bought two. Making eleven in all.'

'I do not wish to be rude in the face of your hospitality. But I must ask the price.'

'The price to me was meaningless. Price. Money.'

'It was in American payment.'

'It was a thousand dollars by each canvas. He was insistent.'

I bet he was insistent, the bastard.

'Herr Siska. Would you estimate for me, only as a generality, what your paintings are worth in the city of Vienna?'

'I visited Vienna once, 1935, think it was. Saw lots of paintings in the galleries across from a palace, but couldn't figure them out. Looked like they'd tried too hard, you know what I mean?'

I don't write on naive art for glossy magazines but even I could guess at Vienna shop prices Westfall was buying Jan Siska's paintings for a thousand and selling for five. A cool $4,000 profit per canvas, and then multiply it by eleven. And all from I Board funds – don't think he was buying them out of his own pocket. $44,000 per year on top of his normal salary and if he kept this up he would be off to an early retirement in the Caribbean.

But he wasn't going to keep it up because now I was in a position to stop him.

'Shall I have Helena bring more wine? Siska asked.

'That would be very kind. And I wish also to say that your police, now or in the future, whatever police they may be, will do you no harm.'

We finished the second carafe together.

Then I left him and walked back toward the waiting Czech automobile. *Clank*, I thought, smiling, the trap for Westfall had finally snapped shut.

Chapter 10

'*Kashmar takoy*! *Nevozmozhno*!' grumbled the Ambassador. 'The Vienna traffic has become without hope.'

Four of us were being chauffeured in great luxury in the Ambassador's Chaika limousine down Rennweg towards Karlsplatz and the Vienna exposition buildings. Chervenkov our *Rezident* and I lounged beside the Ambassador in the back seat, Razin the security chief was up front beside the Red Army sergeant-chauffeur.

'The Austrian traffic authorities could not organise women pushing baby carriages,' said Chervenkov.

'They're all beer drinkers,' piped up Razin. The ladies with baby carriages? I questioned his syntax.

'Then these beer drinkers need our quality Soviet machine tools, no?' The Ambassador was drumming up his enthusiasm for a display of Soviet power lathes and automatic welding equipment. These were to be unveiled at an exposition ingeniously housed in a Habsburg palace facing the art history museum. Maybe I could sneak across to see the Breughels.

'Well Sergei?' growled Chervenkov. He had read my preliminary report but my request for a conference was the reason I was now included in this party driving to the exposition.

'Westfall. I believe we have him.'

'What the hell does "believe" mean? Do you have him or don't you?'

'You move slow,' Razin added. 'How long must we wait upon your complex scheming? You better start to deliver.'

Ignore him.

'Westfall journeys to Brno in Czechoslovakia under the auspices of the I Board as a consultant to a Western engineering corporation. He utilises I Board funds to purchase naive oil paintings. Which he sells on the Vienna market.'

'So what? It's his money?' complained Razin.

'$10,000 outlay?'

'It is not an enormous amount, Sergei. Do not forget we want to break the bastard, not chastise him for dipping into the petty-cash account.'

'Listen to my reasoning: $10,000 in the spread of one year is too high to come from Westfall's own pocket. But it is small enough to escape without suspicion from the American I Board expenses. Undoubtedly he has created a fictitious recipient or agent in Brno to deceive his auditors.'

'What about deceiving his boss, Stillwater, eh?'

'Stillwater has other occupations, Comrade Razin, than auditing expense accounts. He would never know. That is, until Westfall retires prematurely to enjoy his investment.'

'What is the size of the mark-up, his net earning?' Chervenkov, the blunt-headed realist, at least posed professional questions.

'I estimate roughly 5 to 1. That would yield net earnings in excess of $40,000.'

'Not bad, not bad,' harumphed the Ambassador. 'If he were managing a Soviet factory he would receive a productivity bonus. Recruit this Westfall to manage some steel plant in Kursk! Perhaps he could teach our lazy workers to reach their productivity norms!'

I had scored. The Ambassador was not a professional sceptic like my KGB chief Chervenkov.

And he tended to endorse projects without extensive scrutiny. But he would nevertheless influence Chervenkov. I could, however, expect more protest from Razin. Here it came:

'Typically, Sergei has involved us in some woolly plot totally unfounded on concrete—'

'*Bozhe moy*!' bellowed the Ambassador. 'My God! Look at that!'

We were blocked behind a tram in the chaos of Schwarzenbergplatz. Pedestrians streamed across the tracks. It was a hot day. Standing beside the tram stop was a blonde girl in a Tyrolean dirndl exposing glorious breasts with a cleavage as deep as an Alpine valley.

The conversation became carnal.

'140 centimetres!' the Ambassador leered. '140 centimetres at the very minimum!' Say, 40 inches for those Anglo-Americans who have not yet gone metric.

Chervenkov made a crude joke about whether that measurement referred to her bust measurement or another anatomical capacity.

I smiled, thinking how little this sport of street gazing enticed me now that I had my private images of Daria. Daria – dark and polished, glistening bronze, scent of citron and almonds, hot Bulgarian summer, olive trees twisting from rock by roadsides trodden from Roman legions marching to the conquest of Thracian gold. Roman centurions with metal buckles hot to the touch under a southern sun, a thousand years before the Slavs from the Russian marsh streamed across the Balkans. Daria and I. And Olga. Our common Slavic source. St Cyril and bearded priests swinging musk scent censers over a golden crucifix. One and separate. Was this why Daria now so fully possessed me? We Russians with our cabbage borsch, beetroots, vodka, acrid cleaning fluid on the marble steps of ministries, the snow howling on dark Moscow mornings. And Olga. Grey-eyed, the distant, tall Soviet brassière-constrained Olga with her pink nipples and earnest enquiries into macroeconomic planning systems, with the dark-tipped, almond brown curve of Daria, Bulgarian wine, figs ripening in the southern sun, thyme sprouting from warm stones of ruined Thracian palaces, golden tobacco mellowing in the Balkan sun. . .

'Keep your eyes upon the steering, driver!' Razin the bureaucrat instructed our chauffeur.

With a flounce of skirt the Austrian girl of Alpine meadows squeezed between stalled automobiles, avoided a beer truck, escaped the charge of a Honda motorcycle, and safely reached the far side of the asphalt.

'Well then?' the Ambassador sighed portly.

'Westfall, sir,' prompted Razin who had not so much as cast one furtive glance at the maiden in the dirndl.

'Yes, Westfall! Back to business! Very well, Sergei, I understand that both our Rezident and Comrade Razin are somewhat more sceptical than I, but what is it you propose to do?'

'Objectively, there are two missing fragments. One: locate the dealer in Vienna to whom Westfall has re-sold the Jan Siska naive paintings. This, though, is a technicality and one of my technicians has already launched an investigation.'

'You said two fragments.'

'Second: the Westfall bank account.'

'The bank account?'

'It is the key, I believe. Reason: at this stage we could pressure Westfall, or denounce him to his chief Stillwater, but we have no final information as to where he has deposited his illegal earnings. Where? What bank? Vienna? Zurich? Washington? If we approached Stillwater, or higher I Board officials, the American press or even the Vienna gutter tabloids, we would seem little more than rumour-mongers. So I will not proceed with the final phase of this operation until we can cite a bank account number and the size of the cash deposit thereupon.'

'How in hell do you propose that? Driver! The other lane, watch the tram! They come at you like owls from hell!'

We were threading through the immense baroque Karlsplatz which, unfortunately, had been delivered to the tender mercies of Viennese traffic engineers with the resultant similarity to a Japanese Kamikaze run or an American demolition derby.

'Verification of the account may be obtained through a variety of methods,' I continued. 'For example, install a mobile van facing Westfall's bank. Utilise microwave sensors. Record the computerised data when he makes his next banking transaction. Or, alternatively, tap into the computer lines from Westfall's branch bank to the central computer terminal.'

'Totally outrageous!' Razin piped. 'It would cost a fortune! That kind of operation is mounted only in Washington, Bonn or London against the NATO governments!'

That of course I knew. By proposing an overly complex method I had lured Razin into a premature objection. Now I could proceed with a more workable suggestion:

'There are, ah, less expensive methods.'

'Eh now, what methods?' grumbled Chervenkov.

'Two on one. The girl and the fat man. It's what we all learn the second day of espionage training.' What I meant was the old, hoary routine of jamming up to Westfall at the bank counter with several of our operatives. Photography of his bank slips or account books would be required of course. But we could handle that.

The driver swung across the boulevard and entered the massive portal of the exhibition hall. The Ambassador tugged at his necktie knot, wet his fingertips and smoothed back his grey hair.

'Just accomplish it, Sergei. I am uninterested in the details. . .'

'. . . or learn you have been snatched up by the security guards in Westfall's bank,' admonished Razin.

The limousine braked to a halt. Austrians with badges and identity cards scurried toward us. Car doors were opened for our benefit.

'Not a bad suit there, Sergei,' Chervenkov my *Rezident* growled as we stepped out. 'Get that thing in Vienna?'

'Spending expenses on imported English suits, huh?' sniped Razin.

'Actually, no. It was, ah, tailored privately,' I said, flicking a mote of lint from my mohair waistcoat. 'Tailored by Heinz Mohr, Vienna', the discreet tag in the lining stated.

I do not wish to imply that in those days Daria transferred her residence to my apartment. But she spent a great deal of her time there and gradually the flat accumulated a collection of film snips, cans of developing fluid, black and white stills of shadow patterns with which she was particularly fascinated, an electric hair-dryer in the kitchen, assorted Gucci moccasins, dogeared back copies of *Cahiers du Cine-*

ma, and two pairs of white Wrangler cotton jeans hanging up to dry in the bathroom.

Our behaviour was, I confess, totally reckless and irresponsible. I lived in growing concern over denouncement by Razin and his legion of spies and informers. But they were concerned primarily with internal penetration of our security at the embassy. Would he monitor my residence in the outlying district? Were other officials having their conjugal lives spied upon? To lessen the danger of public scandal I maintained my official embassy routine with scrupulous attention to schedule. Daria had her own key to the flat and usually arrived in the evenings.

There she was this evening when I returned from the machine-tool exposition. It was beastly humid. She was stretched full length on the living-room rug, wearing a pair of cut-off denim shorts and a white T-shirt. She was tracing abstract charcoal swirls on a large pad of vellum drawing paper. Flat on her belly with her hair tossed back, the muscles of those long legs glistened like polished amber.

Sweaty and somewhat wilted I ripped off my tie and opened the refrigerator. Empty. No wine. Daria was proving to be a lackadaisical housekeeper.

'Damn it. Bloody somebody should fill the thing up.'

'I'm not bloody somebody!'

'It's like jail!'

'You Soviets would know, Sweetie.'

'Don't mock me, girl. Bread and water. Locked up. We are incarcerated in the house.'

'Hey, you! You're the one who's afraid to poke his nose outdoors!'

She was correct, you know. Grumbling, I slouched around the house. The little love nest with the inventive Daria was most charming. But how long could it be expected to last if we were terrified of discovery by Razin? Get out. We had to get out. Air. Breathe. Escape. We had to have air. We would suffocate. The hottest fire can't burn under a damp blanket. Out. . .

'Very well. I am going to take you, chère Mademoiselle, this instant to a *Heuriger*.'

'A Heuriger! Sergei, how super!' She leapt up like a young colt, sailed her drawing pad through the air to land with a smack on the table, and bounded out of the room to pull on a pair of her white jeans.

There are a lot of things wrong with Vienna but Heurigers aren't one of them. As I understand it some Habsburg granted licences to the local vintners for sale of their new – *heuriger* – wine on the premises of their farmhouses and wine presses at the foothills of the Viennese woods. Today these remain fairly rustic establishments, if just marginally avoiding the creeping urban spread of Vienna. They feature new white wine in quarter-litre mugs, black bread, pickles and cold roast pork, outdoor tables under linden trees, and hefty waitresses in white blouses with cheerfully exposed bosoms.

Most of the elite Heurigers are in the 19th district of Grinzing if one avoids those establishments which have prostituted themselves to the tourist trade. The proprietor of my favourite Heuriger was renowned for his heady wine, boisterous public, and refusal to contract his services to the Vienna tourist organisations. About two hundred people were already there when we entered through massive arches of a gelb-tinted farmhouse. Tables were placed on terraces surrounded by a wicker fence with vineyards on either side. Unfortunately, a building speculator had chewed up a neighbouring vineyard to install sloppily modern duplex apartments but these were partially hidden from view by a hedge of raspberry canes.

It seemed to serve no purpose to place Daria and myself in the central courtyard so I chose a table on an upper terrace near the wicker fence conveniently shadowed by the overhanging lindens.

I went back down to the farmhouse and heaped two plates with sausages, pickles, roast pork, cheese, black bread, paprikas and mustard. Struggling up the gravel walkway I met Daria coming from the lower courtyard.

'The Loo,' she laughed.

The evening air was scented with mown hay. We drank wine and ate pickles and crackly roast pork and snuggled together and became tipsy. I called for more! After the day's heat the cool wine seemed as alluring as a mountain brook. We were, after all, virtually in the darkness. Paying no attention to us, the other Viennese men and their ladies were gobbling away, gossiping and flirting, and tossing choice morsels to their numerous *dackel* who wagged their furry tails in delight.

Daria and I snuggled and ate and were having a wonderful time and got kissy and intimate when the three of them strolled in with all the leisure in the world, entered into a long discussion upon which table to select, then settled with some complicated shuffling of chairs at a table two terraces down below us.

My hackles must have risen like a dog off the leash that has just spotted the dog warden.

'What's the trouble, buddy,' Daria complained as I untangled myself from her and stared at the newly arrived threesome. 'Decided enough's enough daring for one night out in public?'

'I believe we have encountered a slight bit of difficulty,' I said tensely.

'Big deal! So what? Who are they, they don't come

from your embassy?'

I don't believe Daria was naive about my own professional activities. But how deeply should I reveal my knowledge of the opposition? Should I lie outright about the American I Board? Why worry what to tell her? I should be thinking how to get out of here without being detected. . .

'See the large man, there,' I whispered, 'sitting at the head of the table, appears to be lecturing the other two chaps?'

'The one with the red hair and freckles? He's wearing a bow tie?' She rose up on her tiptoes for a peek.

'He's named Leslie Stillwater. He is director of an organisation the Americans have implanted in Vienna.'

'What do you mean implanted?'

'What does he look like to you?'

'I mean, Sergei darling, diplomats and pedigrees and titles are your business, no? He looks like what an American cartoonist would draw if he were drawing a southern politician. He's awfully roly-poly. I can hear his terrible Texas drawl all the way up here.'

'Take a close look at the other two.'

'One of them looks sort of like, you know, a Mexican?'

'There,' I indicated quietly, not daring to speak loud enough to be overheard. 'Next to the roly-poly man, he's wearing a white linen suit.' She tried to stand up again but I drew her back to the table. 'The chap that is dressed so snappily is named Richard Salazar. Mexican-American.' And a courier, back-stairs man, electronics training, moves money around, confidant of Stillwater, I thought quickly, racing through my memory of our dossier on the I Board. Why had Salazar appeared? And why was the boss-man Stillwater ambling around with Salazar in public?

'Who's the third guy? The tall long one?'

'You tell me.'

'Sort of hickey, rough, but not so bad looking, huh? He's dressed himself very suave, very chic, those sandals must come right off the Ponte Vecchio of Firenze.'

It was, naturally, my friend Westfall, completing the I Board trio on its night out at a Vienna Heuriger.

The wine in my throat had turned sour, and sweat popped out on my forehead. Why, with two hundred Heurigers in Vienna, with dozens of *gasthäuser*, innumerable outdoor restaurants, why on this sticky night did Westfall, his I Board boss Stillwater, and Salazar the Mercury-swift courier, arrive to haunt me?

Panic cramped my stomach muscles. I fought to clear my wine-fuzzed vision. What were we going to do? Should I walk past them with a polite nod? Or slither down the gravel path beside their table? No. No. Westfall, as soon has he looked up to the higher terraces and saw us, Westfall would delight in bounding up the path and expose us with a great hoop and holler. We had to get out. How? The fence. Vineyards in the darkness. I could boost Daria over the low fence and we could walk down through the vineyards, past the yard of the duplex apartment house, and out to the street and my automobile. . .

'Does that long American with the scar on his cheek have a girl friend?' Daria leaned forward, her eyes glistening with mischief. Despite my predicament I was curious of her reaction to Westfall.

'He chases Yugoslav girls. He would go mad over you. He has a fixation on dark sinuous girls from the

Balkans.'

'Maybe dark sinuous girls from the Balkans chase him. He's the tall rugged American.'

So we see Westfall the amateur writer and historian of Austerlitz battles now posing as a sophisticated man-about-town. What the hell was I waiting around for? I had to exit. By the most elementary rules of my training I should have abandoned Daria and vanished as soon as the I Board men walked into the courtyard.

I wiped the perspiration from the hair matted across my forehead. For a terrible moment as Stillwater gazed around dreamily I thought I was going to be ill. Wait. They had stood up. Were they walking up to the next terrace? They were gazing around . . . we were going to be seen . . . then Westfall and Salazar ambled towards the farmhouse. Stillwater sat down. Salazar and Westfall were going to the farmhouse to fetch the wine and food. I had to vanish or they would return and corner me.

'But Sergei,' Daria protested as I grasped her arm, lifting her up from the table.

'Now be very quiet and don't protest and do not do anything stupid.'

'I never,' she said frostily, 'never do anything stupid.'

'Then bravo, this is an opportunity to uphold your reputation.'

Calmly I peeled off three hundred schillings, placed them under an empty wineglass, clamped my arm around Daria's waist and lifted her over the wicker fence. I bounded after her into the vineyard and darkness. Quickly I led her down the rows of pruned grape vines until we encountered a ditch and the hedge of raspberry bushes. The damn brambles would have stopped a tank. I blundered forward in the darkness, became entangled, ripped my trousers, and a dog started yapping. Lights flickered in the duplex apartment house below us. Was I to be apprehended for trespassing? Desperately I uprooted two wooden staves from the vineyard, threw them across the briar patch, crushed down the raspberry tangle, and with the strength of panic hoisted Daria up in my arms and bulled my way through the breach I had created in the thorny obstacle.

'Yeeoow!'

A ferocious *dackel* had rushed out of the darkness and planted his little white teeth into my ankle. I shook and kicked, balanced on one foot, holding Daria in my arms while the furry little badger hound hung on with grim determination.

'Little doggie!'

'He's chewing me up! Get him off me!'

Artfully Daria scooped up the little beast, cradled him in her arm until he calmed down, patted him on the head, and set him down on the lawn with his tail wagging. I limped around to ease the sting of his bite.

More shouts erupted. An irate landowner was shining a damn big torchlight around the balcony of his duplex apartment. We made a run for it, broke through a boxwood hedge, crashed through to the sidewalk, sprinted to my automobile and leapt inside. Safe. Safe.

Then something odd occurred. Looking at each other, dishevelled, sweatstreaked, Daria with smudged mascara and me with my torn trousers and smarting dog-bite, we began giggling. Then we laughed. We roared. We fell into each others' arms, rocking with laughter, the tears streaming down Daria's face and my body rocking with hilarity.

'The dog, the dog . . .' Daria was trying to say.

Laughing and hugging, the relief flooding through my sweaty body, wrapped around her in total happiness now that we had evaded the terrors of the night, nothing told me that was the last of the laughing.

Chapter 11

Investigation by our embassy specialists proved that my estimates had been surprisingly close to the actual price Westfall achieved for selling Jan Siska's paintings on the Viennese market.

As the documents laid out on my desk testified, the firm Chytil & Gotsch, GmbH, merchants of a moderately disreputable dealership on the Mexicoplatz by the Danube docks, had inserted a series of Jan Siska oil miniatures into their catalogue during the past twelve months. Calculated into dollars from Austrian schillings, the average sales price equalled $7,500 per canvas. My technicians, led by the plump, blond-haired Syzmanski, had learned from other sources at the Vienna auction halls that traditional profit margins for Mexicoplatz sales averaged thirty per cent. This indicated that Westfall obtained about $5,250 per canvas. The grey-haired naive painter Siska, who laboured in the early morning light until the pains became too severe in his lower back muscles, received $1,000 from the generous Westfall for each composition. With a net profit of $4,250 per painting on eleven works of art, Westfall should have collected a cool $46,750 clearance.

'What happens to the naive paintings after they are sold from Chytil & Gotsch?' I demanded.

Syzmanski had slicked down his hair and donned a three-piece black suit to snoop around the art dealers. He looked like a Viennese antique auctioneer, the seedy type who enjoys great prestige selling off the accumulated possessions of destitute nobility.

'The Chytil manager kept his mouth shut.'

'But what did the respectable firms tell you?'

'The Jan Siska stuff is pretty good, they say. This kind of folk-art junk is a big rage in the West.'

'Syzmanski, I would caution you not to refer to Jan Siska's paintings as junk.'

'Well, whatever it is, everybody is cashing in all the way up the line. They tell me, from Vienna the paintings usually are marketed in Munich or Milano. Or the Japs. The Japanese are big on buying this stuff. Think it's kind of cute.'

I was fascinated to estimate the ultimate mark-up for each Jan Siska canvas. And let me remind you that we Soviets, we communists, we are slandered in the Western press for our heartless exploitation of the weaker members of our societies!

'A capable performance, Syzmanski. Now, please summon the clerk from the finance section. Westfall's . . .'

The telephone buzzed. Damn it. I yanked the thing off the hook. The receptionist stated that someone had called with a request to speak to the economic attaché.

My back stiffened. My contacts in the Austrian business world usually page me by my full name and title.

'Who requests the economics attaché?'

'A young lady, but she said it was urgent.'

I sat up with a bolt.

'Then please connect me,' I said calmly for the benefit of the receptionist as a slight film of chalk began to coat my tongue.

Click.

'Hi, Sergei? I know. You said not to use the telephone.'

It was Daria.

I glanced at Syzmanski who was apparently paying no attention to me as he pruned the cuticle behind his nails with a broken wooden matchstick.

'Perhaps it would be more convenient, *Mein Herr*,' I purred, 'if I could return your call somewhat later . . .'

'Cut it out man!' she yelled in English. 'You going to give me the diplomatic run around?'

My God! If the receptionist was listening. . .

'Well then, perhaps,' I continued to purr, 'if you would be kind enough to indicate a return number to be telephoned. . .'

'Look. Today, huh? There is lots and lots you haven't even started to hear about. . . .'

At that moment a timid knock sounded on my office door. I glanced up, the sweat undoubtedly shining on my forehead. In walked the female clerk from the finance section. Desperately straining to control my panic I motioned her to take a seat.

'Very good then,' I continued with Daria. 'May I suggest the usual, at 5:00pm?' I wanted to get Daria the hell off the embassy telephone line and meet her in the flat to determine if she had lost all reason.

'No way! I want to see you at the Big Mac. Three at the latest, OK?'

I mumbled something diplomatically appropriate and with my perspiration-slick hand cradled the telephone. Let me tell you this: the lowest probational recruit, had he been listening casually to Daria's insane telephone conversation, the most naive intelligence trainee would know she was waiting for me at McDonalds hamburgers on the Schwarzenbergplatz at 1500 hours.

'You wanted the money clerk,' Syzmanski prompted me dutifully. I could barely concentrate on what he was saying. I felt totally wilted. The kneecaps of my suit were stained through with perspiration. The most important question was to determine whether our embassy telephone recording devices had intercepted Daria's irresponsible conversation. Normally we did not record individual inquiries. But standard instructions could be modified by the security chief, Razin. Did he now have a tape recording of our conversation? I could be ruined. If that call had been monitored . . .

'You have been summoned,' I turned smoothly to the finance clerk, 'to inquire about various interest rates within the Austrian banking system.'

'Interest rates depend on how liquid an account is intended to be,' the girl clerk said accurately.

'What does liquid mean?' questioned Syzmanski with a faint reek of fish.

'Liquid signifies quick cash,' she replied. She then described that the Austrian banks, as banks everywhere, offered various interest rates depending whether cash could, or could not, be withdrawn on demand. A savings programme which was based on purchase of Austrian government bonds would command high rates but could not be retrieved at the stroke of a pen, she continued to explain.

'What if one required an account where a large sum could be put in and taken out with quick turnover?'

'Then you would use a *sparbuch*, a savings' book plan,' the finance clerk answered. I studied her closely. She was a petite girl with nondescript blonde hair and big blue eyes magnified by her large spectacles. Her brown suit was buttoned up rigidly to the collar. She could have been accepted in any central European city from Minsk to Warsaw to Vienna. I began to include her in my calculations.

'And your name, comrade?'

'Anna Ivanova Komorova,' she answered promptly. Anna Ivanova appeared to be the model clerk, I thought. Well-trained, disciplined, though not wholly unattractive. Feet solidly on the ground. Not stupid enough to be seduced by some Western agent-gigolo.

'Well then, Anna Ivanova,' I said in my best avuncular bass, 'just what type of account would a Western intelligence agent employ if he wanted to house illegally obtained earnings?'

'Again, it would be a *sparbuch* account,' she replied enthusiastically. I could see financial transactions fascinated Anna Ivanova. 'That is because he might wish a quick transfer to a foreign bank. Your agent would use a *sparbuch* with *losungswort* system for withdrawals.'

It was opportune to demonstrate my understanding of Austrian banking mechanisms:

'By a *losungswort* he, the Western agent, would present his savings book to the bank teller. Write the code word on a slip of paper. Present this to the bank teller who had inserted the *sparbuch* in the mechanical intake of the accounting computer.'

'Yes. Exactly. They are using a Philips computer at most of the Vienna banks. It has a visual screen which verifies the *losungswort* – code word – when the teller types out the account number.'

'And if the *losungswort* on the computer screen matches the code word written on the paper slip, the bloke gets his cash.'

'Correct. It's fast,' beamed Anna Ivanova through her spectacles.

I swivelled around to face Syzmanski.

'Could you work it with Anna Ivanova?'

'A couple of rehearsals would be necessary. Yeah. It would be pretty routine as long as we know the general bank setup.'

'With me?' asked Anna Ivanova. 'I am not permitted to leave the finance section without official clearance.'

'Then you shall obtain such clearance. Comrade Syzmanski will explain exactly how to run the sequence in the bank. Syzmanski, I want it all on film.'

'Not difficult, but we'll need a third stand-off with a camera.'

'I authorise it. I want to film the action at the counter. We must be certain Westfall is unaware of what we are doing to him.'

There were other details. We knew Westfall used a branch of the Creditanstaltbankverein in the third district. We did not have the luxury of knowing when he would choose to make his next visit to the bank. This would require permanent surveillance of his apartment during banking hours with Syzmanski and Anna Ivanova immobilised within our embassy. They must be prepared to be driven to the bank on short notice as soon as it became evident that Westfall intended to make a deposit or withdrawal. I did not like the uncontrolled loss of time that would be involved, but I consoled myself with the fact that this was the last step required. With a secure documentation of Westfall's account number and the size of his deposit, we would be finally in a position to launch our punitive operation.

We adjourned for tea and sandwiches at the embassy canteen then continued discussion on the technical problems which still faced us. I finished with Syzmanski and Anna Ivanova at 2:00pm, promptly informed the receptionist that I would not return for the afternoon and left the embassy on foot to the nearby Schwarzenbergplatz. No car. The last thing I could afford would be to have my Lada booked for illegal parking outside McDonalds hamburgers.

I went through a few standard pavement exercises

to determine if I was being followed. The abrupt-halt-before-a-shop-window routine. Nothing. No reflections. The reversed course, turn around, walk back up the sidewalk ploy. Zero. No one darted away or ducked down side streets. The jump one tram, jump off, board another gambit. Zero again. No scurrying feet to catch up. I breathed somewhat easier, although for all I knew every teeny, school age, hamburger-gulping Austrian punk in the horrible, horrible, garish, plastic McDonalds could be fully employed as an American – or Soviet – agent, to catch me in my delinquency with the stunning Daria.

It was 3:00pm and the despicable establishment was jammed to the rooftops. Neon lights reflected dizzily from the red and yellow plastic table tops, Austrian school girls, American tourists, Afro-Asian students, and back-packing Britons jostled in long lines to purchase pimple-producing chocolate milkshakes and chloresterol-count hamburgers. Since the franchise owner with his three hundred per cent profits had not seen fit to install proper air conditioning the scent of closely packed bodies mixed delicately with the odour of hissing grease.

Shoved, bumped with the sharp edge of plastic trays, jostled about, I carefully sought out Daria among the masses. Finally I spied her wedged into a two-seat table in a far corner adjacent to a booth occupied by an Austrian family of six soulfully licking drippy ice-cream cones.

Daria was wearing her white Wrangler jeans, Pierre Cardin sunglasses, and a blue T-shirt which said *Dallas Cowboys.* Her hair was jerked up and tied in a bun. This seemed to draw back the flesh along the high cheekbones and made her look rather Levantine, tense and unpredictable.

'Ciao, buddy, we have troubles,' she said with a toss

of her head.

'We will have many more troubles if we do not leave this terrible place. Do you know—'

'No lectures please, Sergei my friend. Play the experienced man of action. Keep a cool head. Put on your diplomatic sang froid. 'Cause you got to tell me what to do. Fast. Very fast.'

Daria was pregnant, I thought feverishly. I had made Daria pregnant. Being mature, we had of course taken certain. . . doctors, I racked my brain for medical specialists who would prove amenable, confidential, not linked to the diplomatic community but free to perform private practice and not encumbered by the time-consuming restrictions of the Autrian state medical system. Of course, if she wished to keep the child, I would act honourably and responsibly. The most important thing was to ascertain exactly what she wanted. We had to do this calmly. In that respect she was completely correct in her lecture about keeping calm. But to speak of Daria's pregnancy across chocolate milkshakes in this horrible American establishment? How utterly inappropriate. . .

'Listen, Daria,' I said evenly. 'You can trust me to be reasonable. But this is hardly the place to discuss something confidential.'

'It's gotta do.'

Losing my touch I blurted out:

'You're pregnant.'

She whipped off her sunglasses, shook her head and laughed softly.

'My God, I wish I was, Sergei, I wish I was. It would be so much simpler.'

Chapter 12

'Daddy's got to go home.'

I suddenly felt out of my depth. My vision wavered and I had difficulty hearing her over the racket. Perfectly capable of dealing with defecting code men on late night Vienna streets I seemed unable to keep abreast of Daria in the grease-popping heat of an American hamburger franchise.

'I don't understand you.'

'Daddy. My father. The Ambassador. Can you understand that Sergei sweetie?'

I nodded my head slowly.

'Ambassador Kaladzhiev. Head man of the Bulgarian embassy. My father. Good party member and the whole bit. Somewhat unexpectedly and ahead of normal rotational schedules, but apparently with no censure or pejorative implication, he is being recalled to Sofia. In fact, hooray,' she twirled the sunglasses around her finger, 'he is receiving a promotion.'

With the scent of a *fischMac* clotting my nostrils I asked her very dryly, 'When is he being recalled?'

'Oh, there is lots of time.'

'Six months?'

'Who the hell do you think he is working for? The United States Department of State? The British Foreign Office? When the Bulgarians say come home they mean come home.'

'So, when?'

'In exactly three weeks. Neat. The foreign ministry has already booked the tickets.'

Only now did I begin to realise what Daria was

talking about and why we were sitting on plastic-backed chairs and why she meant it was urgent and what it was going to do to my life.

'You said tickets?'

'Yes tickets. Plural. Two. More than one. One for Daddy the Ambassador.'

'And one for you.'

'Right on the nose. Go to the head of the class. One ticket is for me.'

I like to think of myself as a solid, sober individual but I suddenly wanted something strong to drink, something a lot stronger than McDonald's with its All American beverages could offer. I pushed up to the counter and to keep my mind from what Daria had said I ordered a cup of coffee. Thin, vile liquid. That's the way it is, I thought, act on your appetites and break the rules and if you are particularly clever you will not be punished but you can lose in any case and it does not matter if you are censured officially or destroy your private life but the things that count are taken away from you. They are taken away because it is foolish to believe you can control the permanence of relations that cause you true happiness. No, that is incorrect, you can control any relationship, but it takes leverage and influence and for all my relative authority I was not certain of my power to alter the decrees of the Bulgarian diplomatic service and its recalls of its ambassadors. Which meant in less than one month Daria would be flown back to Sofia and there were damn few excuses which I could devise to place myself in Sofia and I knew somehow vaguely I might survive it as an adult but I had no idea how I could deal with the hole that would be ripped out of my life when she went away from me.

I wandered back and watched her drinking her chocolate milkshake through a waxed paper straw.

'I was questioning, Daria, whether or not you are making this too complicated. Could you simply place a request with your authorities to continue your studies in Vienna?'

'Are you totally unreal? If I start throwing around bright ideas like that they'll put me on the first airplane tomorrow morning.'

'You are not being logical.'

'Get that official frosty tone out of your voice.'

'They have already given you permission to reside in the West. It can be extended.'

'Not with Daddy back home it won't! He goes back, I go back!'

'What the hell were you telling me at your embassy cocktail party?'

'Please release your grip on my wrist, muscle man.'

'. . . about going back to Bulgaria and working in the textile mills? About true art and dedication?'

'Don't be tiresome, Sergei. That was a cocktail party and both of us were engaging in something of a flirt.'

'So, it's *aufwiedersehen* baby?'

'There's not going to be any *aufwiedersehen*. At least, to be technical, not as far as my Bulgarian motherland might be concerned.'

That hit me like she had socked me in the pit of my stomach. The air rushed from my lungs as I stared at her with my pulse pounding heated and feverish.

'I am not returning to the Peoples' Republic of Bulgaria, sweetheart,' she said tightly. 'Let me put it even clearer: I want to defect to the West. I want to renounce my citizenship. But there are costs involved and danger and I do not have the resources to do it alone.'

She paused, apparently to let me draw the appropriate conclusion. I fought to control the nervous paralysis which had locked a crab claw across my chest. I sensed my strength erode as quickly as wind lifts sand and scatters it across the sea. I simply felt incapable of facing the demand with which Daria had now confronted me. I was currently engaged, at this point in time, in a highly sensitive operation against an intelligence operative of the United States government. If it could not be said that I bore direct responsibility to the Soviet people or the Russian nation for the Westfall operation, then it remained true that I bore an obligation to my professional career service to discharge my duty with the utmost attention and concern for detail. I could not allow myself to be drawn into tangential affairs, however personal or emotionally demanding they might appear.

'What you are saying is that you want me to assist you.'

With her tongue Daria Kaladzhiev licked the chocolate ice cream from the end of the straw.

'Take it or leave it. But the odds are about 99.95 per cent that I can't make it without you. Is that realistic enough for your taste?'

As the Pakistani table boy took away our trays I thought of the white trace of Daria's swimsuit along her tanned body, the citron scent which pervaded the room on warm mornings when she left me, the smear of her tear-stained eyes as we laughed with my torn trousers when the dog bit me escaping from the *heuriger*.

Slowly, bowed with worry, I nodded my head: '*Da*.'

'Yes? You know exactly what it is you are doing?'

'*Da*, very well, yes, I accept,' I told her.

'Consequences? You understand the consequences to you personally and your private responsibility?'

'Yes, Daria,' I said tiredly, reached over and broke in half the milkshake straw. 'I completely understand the consequences.'

A lot later in the evening I jumped from a tram on the Mexicoplatz beside the Danube barge docks and walked in the direction of Chytil & Gotsch art merchants. The firm's display window was packed with Romanian ikons, bronze censers, folk carvings and wooden church panels smuggled up the river by barge crewmen. Somebody was making a rakeoff, judging by the exorbitant price tags, but I concluded that the profits went up the Danube, not down it.

Sited alone in a corner niche was a tiny canvas mounted on wood backing which bore the unmistakably precise brushmarks of Jan Siska. It portrayed a group of men in black suits and women in dark shawls returning through a field of ripe wheat from a walled graveyard on the far horizon, while superimposed in distorted scale were storks and waterfowl nesting among reeds and rushes. Death and continuity, but I am not sure Jan Siska needed to formulate his concepts or develop elaborate theories before he began to work at his easel in the early mornings. For the rest of us it was not so simple and my own creations, however malevolent by comparison to Siska's, required considerable technical formulation and now I was burdened with two of them.

For I had the obligation to conclude our punishment of the I Board's Westfall while, virtually simultaneously, within the space of three weeks, I had to achieve that most difficult of operations – a political defection. I could not allow the second operation to compromise the first, but I could not become so absorbed with my conclusion of the Westfall assignment that I had no energy remaining to insure Daria's safe removal from the control of the Bulgarians. This left a zero margin for error. It was going to be very difficult and the penalties for mistakes would be instant and absolute.

I stared at the Siska miniature, trying to drain the confusion from my body. I needed to achieve a sense of quiet, and retreat from fear and worry of personal danger to deal with two incredibly intertwined operations with complete objectivity. First I attempted to establish the current time sequence. The I Board assignment was nearing completion, my obligation for Daria was only now beginning. But Daria's time limitations were absolute, Westfall's still relative. I knew the deadline for Daria, but with Westfall we were dependent on his time-decision to approach his bank.

Daria's first requirement was to find a domicile beyond the immediate grasp of the Bulgarian authorities. That could be Austria, as a neutral state, but I wasn't sure about it. I wanted to keep her near me. But my own preferences could not be allowed to shape that fundamental point. The second consideration was money. Daria would not need to languish as a penniless refugee, but the initial stages needed cash backing. Whose cash? I mentally pigeonholed that question and passed to the next point – our visible relationship. Daria must vacate my flat, as unpleasant for me as that might prove. We would both be compromised if she were detected there and after her defection my career would be crushed if it could be established that we had been living there together in Olga's absence.

I then separated Daria's problem from Westfall, broke it into separate categories of objective, execution, and logistics. Walking back through the dusty streets of the second district I formulated a course of action but it was only one course I could follow among several alternatives. One point was immediately clear to me: the time frame was entirely too short. Three weeks were meaningless. We needed two or three months and I didn't have them. This increased the pressure on me enormously, forced me to take arbitrary decisions and base the planning on guesses and pure luck. We had only twenty-one days and I needed every one of them and still I did not think it was going to be enough.

I finally returned to the embassy with dirt-stained shirt collar and scuffed shoes and knew that I needed to work throughout the night to keep abreast of my immediate deadlines. Settling into my desk, I cradled my head in my hands, shut my eyes and tried to draw the reserves of strength I had always been able to command but now needed in double doses.

It was only much later, sorting through the telex messages that had accumulated in my dispatch tray, that I noticed a message our signals centre should have hand-carried to me directly.

For, according to the telex from our Ministry of Foreign Affairs, Ing. G. V. Sokolovskiy was attending an intra-CMEA petroleum conference in Budapest and had requested my presence if it were not inconvenient.

Inconvenience was not the issue since Soviet Minister of Petroleum and Mining Sokolovskiy was my father-in-law. But this summons could not have come at a more difficult time. My resolve to carry my dual responsibilities was nearly crushed under this new complication. For in my anxiety over Daria I had neatly suspended the other half of my personal life which happened to be comprised of a wife, son and father-in-law.

Finally, wearily, I rang the duty receptionist and told her to book a flight reservation on Malev to Budapest for tomorrow, but it was past midnight and tomorrow was today.

Chapter 13

The slap of a wet mop woke me up. It was seven in the morning and I had been sleeping face down on the desk. My mouth tasted foul and my clothing was begrimed. I shook my head dizzily, grasped the edge of the desk for support, pushed myself up and slouched down the hall to our executive washroom to shave. Staring back at me from the mirror two yellowed eyes glinted dully above a sallow face and spiky beard. Any casual acquaintance could realise that I was suffering severe strain. It was impossible to continue with this beaten, hang-dog expression. I had to pull myself together or Razin and the other intelligence officials would begin to question whether I could fulfil my assignments. Shutting off the hot water I threw myself into a frigid shower, changed into clean linen and dressed in my Heinz Mohr tailored mohair suit.

As I walked back to my office I decided I must start taking decisions. Daria should make her initial defection in Switzerland, I concluded. The Bulgarians probably would not hesitate to grab her and crash over the border to Hungary or Czechoslovakia if she remained in Austria, but the logistics of a snatch operation would be more complex if she asked for asylum in Switzerland.

Money. I could not count on the Swiss to be particularly generous with the hand-outs. Eventually, of course, with her Nikon camera and artistic talents she could pay her own way. But she needed a limited fund of instant capital. Could I secure cash for her in

Switzerland? Would our officials in the Bern embassy notice a transfer on the Vienna embassy account to a Swiss bank?

I had no answer. The money had to be made available. If there was enough time I could concoct an excuse for a flying visit to Swiss banks and establish a mechanism for a cash transfer which would be difficult to detect. Twenty-one days. Twenty days. There was no time.

As I grappled with technical issues the staff bus drove into the embassy courtyard. This was the bus which transports those employees who do not have permission to live individually in Vienna but are housed instead in a Soviet-owned apartment block. Peeping out of my window, I watched Razin step onto the gravel courtyard, followed by two or three code clerks and the girl finance clerk Anna Ivanova. Anna Ivanova. That forced my decision. It was a snap shot, as the Americans would say, firing from the hip but it was the best I could do.

I packed my flight bag for the trip to Budapest and waited cautiously for Anna Ivanova to reach the finance section. Then, carefully scanning the corridor for Razin, I hurried to the security door, tapped out the correct combination on the electric lock and stepped inside the vault.

'Good morning, pretty ladies!'

Three of the finance girls were sitting by a Western-style coffee urn, gossiping about men and boy friends. Anna Ivanova sprang up like a jack-in-the-box, blushing as red as a turnip. She was dressed in a chaste white blouse with a big silk bow and pleated blue skirt. The other girls scattered in a titter of confusion and I had her all to myself. I turned on the Uncle Sergei bass voice:

'Well now, Anna Ivanova, how does it go?'

'Very well indeed,' she said enthusiastically, her blue eyes sparkling behind those big lens glasses. 'Comrade Syzmanski and I have practised exactly what it is I am to do at the bank and we now must be patient and wait, he says. Do you believe it is going to take a very long time?'

'Now now. We shall see. You have my utmost confidence.'

'Why thank you,' she said primly.

'Anna Ivanova,' I continued with grave formality, 'given the circumstances of this assignment which occupies my full efforts, I wish to make advance payment to my Klagenfurt account.'

I referred, of course, to the financial incentives which I provided to certain useful contacts in the southern Austrian province on the border of Yugoslavia who were completely independent of the Westfall operation.

'Why, how advanced?'

'Six months.'

'Oh, that is good because anything of a greater time requires special clearance.'

I knew that. That was why I specified six months. I did not want Anna Ivanova asking for special clearance, since I intended to filch this money – which had been intended for my south Austrian operation – for the immediate needs of Daria Kaladzhieva.

Anna Ivanova quickly typed out the administrative forms and pushed the smooth brown sheets across the desk for my signature. I intended to cash the funds at my convenience the day before Daria's exile in Switzerland.

'This of course is a *Losungswort* system, exactly like the one you and Syzmanski will monitor here in Vienna?'

'Yes.'

'It is?'

Give me the code word woman! I nearly shouted. Without the *Losungswort* I could not obtain this cash for Daria.

'Of course,' she said without further elaboration.

'Now, for example,' I continued calmly, my eyes pounding behind my rising blood pressure, 'what *Losungswort* would the recipients of this morning's transfer need to furnish the bank in order to obtain this particular cash payment?'

'Well, I am not so certain. You see, the code word is in the files.'

Obviously she wished not to prove uncooperative, but she wasn't going to blab out the code word. Against all my conservative instincts I had to shoot wildly like some American Wild West cowboy.

'Could you not inform me, simply as an example,' I stated heavily, 'what type of code words are utilised under the Austrian system?'

That was a totally idiotic sentence but Anna Ivanova trotted off to the files to locate the bank code word.

She came back in three minutes with a big smile on her face. 'The *Losungswort* for your transaction is "*butterbrot*".'

'"*Butterbrot*"?'

'Yes, it is "*butterbrot*". Sometimes they use their imaginations,' she beamed innocently.

Butterbrot. '*Buttered bread*'. But I was going to use that code word a lot sooner than the intended recipients and it was not going to be in Austria's southern provinces, if my plans developed correctly. I took a very deep breath to calm my throbbing pulse.

'A *Losungswort* code word can be used at any of the particular bank's branches?'

'Why yes, of course,' she beamed.

'Anywhere in Austria?' I intended to cash it here in Vienna.

'That is the way it can be done.'

'You are very cooperative, Anna Ivanova.'

'Thank you, sir. You see, for a clerk in the finance section, this is all very exciting,' she smiled and blinked those big blue eyes.

Malev Hungarian airlines departed on the button at 17:15 in the afternoon. In actuality I should have driven to Budapest, had I the energy. The flight lasted only about thirty-five minutes and that was protracted enough since we were flying a Soviet Tupolev. I've been spoiled with the abundant seat space and luxury of American-manufactured aircraft.

A hot summer twilight curled over the Hungarian capital. Diamonds of light winked out of the gathering blue haze and the lights of the parliament buildings by the Danube blazed like a gilded necklace. From the sweeping spires of St Mathias cathedral on Buda hill to the dazzle of the lights on the Danube bisecting the city, I realised again what even the Viennese would admit with little hesitation, that Vienna cannot compete with Budapest on a summer night.

A Hungarian protocol official whisked me through customs control and summoned a chauffeur for the drive to the Soviet ambassador's residence. The air was scented with coffee and paprika and spitted pork and the night blazed with lights along the river. All of Budapest seemed to be strolling in the night air. Perhaps the tourist board had concocted it for my benefit, but a tinkle of zither and accordion danced in the blue evening across the water on Margaret Island.

Long lines of official Mercedes and Volgas were parked outside the Soviet ambassador's residence. I had anticipated that any meeting of our socialist economic bloc petroleum ministers would necessitate festive relaxation, thus I was fully prepared for the cocktail party that was in progress as I entered the ornate building.

About one hundred men occupied the banquet hall. Every Eastern European race was represented from the erect, silver-templed East German petroleum minister to the curly-locked Romanian state secretary for petroleum resources and swarthy Magyar minister of transport. A certain decorum was being observed, conversation was polite but not spirited and the Soviet-catered hors d'oeuvres were being consumed with considerable gravity. No particular joy reigned since, I guessed, the distinguished ministers had been squabbling throughout the day about petroleum deliveries and we Soviets had some of it and the rest – excepting the gypsyite Romanians – had almost none at all.

My father-in-law was speaking with the Polish ambassador, thus I chatted diplomatically with some Romanian coal and methane specialists and served myself an impromptu supper. It was only later in the evening as the chauffeured limousines began to crunch on the raked gravel drive that Ing. Sokolovskiy nodded in my direction and slipped through a French door into an adjoining study. I followed after the lapse of a discreet three minutes.

'Hello Papa!'

'Sergei!' He embraced me and kissed me on both cheeks with loud smacks.

Ing. Sokolovskiy was a thickset man with strong neck, flaring white eyebrows and white hair brushed back rather romantically as though he entertained secret longings to serve as an orchestra director in his next incarnation. It was easy to see that Olga had taken her distant grey-flecked eyes from her father. But this sternness was offset by a Saint Nicholas-like rosy blush to his cheeks, and by his burly, back-slapping manners and chuckle.

'And how is the Doctor?'

'Damn it, I tell you not to refer to my titles!'

Papa Sokolovskiy had a doctorate in mathematical science, but he never added this appendage to his title.

'If you were an Austrian you would be calling yourself Herr Doctor Engineer!'

'Then thank God I am not an Austrian!' he chuckled. 'Just call me Comrade Engineer. Here, sit down and have a drink.'

He sloshed a very hefty portion of embassy Ballentine's twelve-year whisky into my glass. Nothing at the residence was second-rate, I had to concede. The walls of the study were panelled with deep polished walnut. The old leather Biedermeier chairs had obviously been removed from some Hungarian bourgeois home upon the arrival of the Red Army in Budapest in 1944. The mahogany desk beside us bore art nouveau engravings and the brass lamp and amber lampshade were fine products of 1920's art deco. It was a wonderful room in which one could drink whisky, listen to the sounds of the summer evening through the open French windows and talk long into the night of our homes far away.

We talked about the Vienna embassy and my general assignment there and where I desired my next posting. Yes, I conceded, I believed that I would continue to be most effective in a foreign-based assignment. My personal preference was for a return to London or Washington. And his career?

'Stable, Sergei, my Lord, it could not be more stable. Ha! European ministers of state would envy my official longevity! No capitalist politician could grasp the utter immobility of our system. There is not the slightest current for change or adventure. The planning system is all-sacred. Our means of relating supply to demand are beyond inquisition. From the ranks of our hallowed academies comes not the slightest intelligent proposal for structural improvement.'

'You sound like some wild-eyed youth of seventeen.'

'Somebody must raise his voice in protest! What have I to lose but my ministry? I can tell you cases of bureaucratic stupidity which the Western propaganda organs would blush to print!'

'Don't exaggerate. You cannot deny that our economy provides constant social services which are admirable.'

'Aye. Humph,' he snorted, swallowing his whisky like a ship captain, 'constant services. Very constant. Housewives still queue for melons in Moscow on the same streetcorners they queued in 1930! We have poured billions of rubles into our socialised farms. With what result? Peasants with private plots the size of a bedsheet still provide eighty per cent of all eggs and vegetables. My cook buys oranges from a peasant who flies to Moscow from the Crimea, pays his fare with his earnings, and still makes a hundred per cent profit!'

'You are turning negativist in your old age.'

'You come back home to Moscow from your luxurious Western existence. We'll see who'll be negativist, damn you!' he laughed, the blood rushing to his cheeks.

We laughed and argued and at the end of it amid all the joking I began to express the silent hope that no one had switched on the recording devices.

'What the hell's going on with you and Olga?' he bellowed suddenly.

I stood up and walked to the china cabinet to study a well-wrought silver service which, to judge the method by which the silver handles had been cast in vine patterns, must have dated from the *sezession* period of 1900.

'Apparently she is much absorbed with her academic obligations.'

'Don't give me that frigid evasion stuff! Are you two speaking to one another?'

'She chooses not to write. It was exactly like this for the last six or seven months before her departure.' I opened the cabinet and studied the silversmith's mark on a silver pitcher to determine whether it originated in Vienna or Budapest. 'I do not wish to allege that Olga has not dealt with me fairly and with correct deportment.'

'Deportment my God! You are a married couple not some debating society!'

'Deportment, Papa. She performed the duties of the household, was a correct partner for me at my official receptions, but twenty-three hours a day it was the dissertation and the textbooks. What more do you wish me to say?'

Papa Sokolovskiy could be crude when he so chose:

'Were you sticking your hand up your secretary's skirt?'

'*Nyet*,' I answered most truthfully.

'It's we Sokolovskiys,' he grumbled. 'We decide a particular objective is important. Then nothing else is of importance, save obtaining that objective. I decided I wanted to be a member of the Central Committee and I utilised all possible means to be elected a member of the Central Committee.'

'How many years did that consume?'

'Fifteen years, son. As I say, things move slow in our stable Soviet society.'

I sat down gloomily, and, I suppose, somewhat guilt-ridden for my behaviour with Daria. Daria. Whose defection . . . in nineteen days . . . the cash advance by the *losungswort*, would it be enough to provide for her residence in Switzerland?

'I'm sorry, you were saying?'

'Answer me! Are you going to stay married to the woman!'

Shamefully for the first time in weeks I was forced to confront my emotional bonds with Olga. We had been very young and our first contacts incredibly Puritan in the marble-halled spaces of the university with no lodging of our own to escape to, forced to court one another with a chaste holding of hands on stairways outside the door of Ing. Sokolovskiy's apartment. And later, Olga standing beside me, tall and erect with those distant cool grey eyes deflecting the gossip and spite and intrigue of a hundred bone-dry cocktail receptions, worrying with me through my promotions and struggle with my foreign languages and assignments I in reality was too young to receive but had performed credibly through my own talents, but due as much I realised now to her quiet confidence.

'Well, dammit?'

'Yes, yes of course it is my wish to remain always with Olga.' And that was the second time in two days I had said *Da* to a question of trust and morality.

It was very late when he rose to return to his quarters. We had emptied the Ballentine's.

'You are having your name printed all over the capitalist newspapers,' I remarked.

'So I am informed. It is because I authorised a contract with British Petroleum.'

'It was true that this was your doing?'

'Of course it was true. I had little choice.' He was standing with his hands clasped behind his back, staring out into the fragrant night from the open window. 'We needed deep water drilling technology. Our Tyumen fields in Siberia have reached their peak outflow. There are other fields up there, but they are less promising than Tyumen, and the investment costs in pipeline are enormous. So terrifyingly costly that the American Alaskan pipeline is as cheap as bread in comparison. I was determined to increase our drilling capacity.'

'But why the English? Why did you sign the contract with British Petroleum?'

'Technical and commercial incentives, Sergei. My specialists were impressed with British experience in their own North Sea drilling programme. I admit to you that we lack the skills to do deep-water exploration. There are large reserves in the Azov and the Caspian, not to say the Pacific basin also, which I believe are more economic to develop than this damn freezing Siberian oil.'

'And British Petroleum is essential for your deep probes?'

'We can't get down there if we don't contract with them.'

'And they wanted petroleum, not money?'

'They are getting a hell of an amount of technical service money. Plus I am selling them 10 million tons of petroleum each year very cheap. Seven per cent below OPEC rates. But that was satisfactory to our Foreign Trade Ministry since the preferential petroleum sale brought down the general cost of the British engineering fees.'

'It said in the newspapers that the Americans were complaining.'

'Of course they were complaining! They are still complaining! I had impressive executives from Texas and California all over my ministry telling me the British could not meet their drilling responsibilities. And the Americans wanted ten per cent price discounts on 25 million tons, carried in American tankers for refining in Galveston, Texas. And those Texans did not hesitate to offer disgusting financial incentives to my subordinates to support the American contract.'

'Swiss bank account incentives.'

'$25,000 cash payments, total $125,000, for five of my top advisers. Who immediately – and dutifully, I am proud to say – denounced the attempted American corruption.'

'So in retaliation, the US denounces you for favouritism and technical error in selecting the British.'

'I should say that neither I, nor anyone connected with one Ing. Sokolovskiy, is particularly admired by the Americans at this moment,' he harumphed.

I joined him by the window and we watched the first streak of red dawn slit the night sky.

Chapter 14

My return flight landed in Vienna at one in the afternoon. Traffic delayed my drive into the city and it was 2:30 before I reached the embassy but when I got there the office was hissing like a samovar.

I rang the technician Syzmanski on the intercom.

'What's going on?'

'We snapped him! Grabbed him like the fox sneaking out of the woods. . .'

'Snapped who, dammit!'

'Westfall went to his bank at 8:30. Anna Ivanova and me. Rush. Reached the bank. Westfall was in line to make a withdrawal. . .'

'Did you get it filmed?'

The telephone rattled. It was my chief, Chervenkov:

'Get in here immediately!'

'Syzmanski,' I yelled, 'did you have it filmed?'

'That is what I try to tell you. It's on film and photocopied and the prints are going to Chervenkov.'

I glanced into the mirror, tightened my cravat, yanked at my cuffs to expose a centimetre of white Oxford shirt cuff and strode with assurance toward Chervenkov's office.

'So you showed up?' the *Rezident* growled. I nodded without comment. In the claustrophobic office Syzmanski had been summoned to mount a portable moving-picture screen and film projector. Another technician ran in with a can of film, fresh, so fresh I could sniff the scent of the developing chemicals.

‘Get it going,’ Chervenkov commanded.

Razin sneaked in. I sat on one of Chervenkov’s cast-iron chairs. Syzmanski had difficulty threading the limp film through the projector. Chervenkov started swearing.

‘Perhaps it is overexposed, and we see nothing,’ Razin complained.

I said nothing. Syzmanski uncapped the lens cover, extinguished the overhead light and switched on the projector.

Blurred black-and-white film flickered on the screen. No sound. Inside of a bank. Marble columns, girl clerks behind the counters, two cashiers’ desks shielded by glass partitions. Potted plants, neon lights, typewriters, girls, paper. Clients. Four men and a woman queued in front of the cashier’s partition. The camera fuzzed, wavered, came back into focus. Westfall was chatting with one of the girl clerks. He was in his blue jeans, Lacoste shirt and sandals. Antics. He was performing a mime. The clerk began to giggle. He held his hands apart, 15 centimetres, palms inward. She grasped his wrist and shortened the distance.

‘What is the bastard doing with the girl?’

‘He’ll lean over and pinch her leg.’

‘What the hell does he say, Sergei?’

‘He is demonstrating his trout fishing.’

‘That’s conjecture.’ Razin dragged on one of his foul cigarettes, the smoke hanging densely in the stale air.

Westfall stepped back from the counter, locked his elbow and brought his forearm forward sharply.

‘That is called Lesson One in the art of fly casting, Comrade Razin.’

Razin started to protest but stopped in mid-sentence as Westfall plucked a rolled piece of tissue paper from his jeans pocket, uncovered a small trout fly and handed it to the girl. Flustered, giggling, she had difficulty with the typewriter keys but eventually typed out a bank statement. He leaned on the counter and signed his name, touched his forehead and turned to stand in line at the cashier's desk.

'Put it on slow motion.'

Syzmanski switched the speed just as a demure Anna Ivanova emerged ghostly from the left side of the frame and inserted herself in the client queue immediately ahead of Westfall. She placed a large leather handbag on the cashier's marble counter and extracted a *sparbuch*, savings book, which the cashier took and inserted into the maw of the Philips computer. Anna Ivanova promptly dropped a ball-point pen. Then she dropped a lipstick tube. So flustered you could detect her blush on the black-and-white film, she turned to Westfall and apologised. He waved his arms around demonstratively, grinned and retrieved the pen and lipstick.

'Very good, very good.'

'He thinks she's some dumb blonde.'

Back she turned to the cashier to retrieve her savings book. The cashier looked past her to Westfall. He stepped forward to the partition, Anna Ivanova moved to one side of the counter, exactly parallel with Westfall who was leaning through the partition to chat with the cashier.

'Slower!'

'There's just this speed, or faster.'

'Watch Syzmanski,' I commented, since Syzmanski had appeared from the bottom of the screen and wedged himself tightly behind Westfall. Then with a hefty shove of his rotund belly he lurched into the American. Westfall whirled angrily. Anna Ivanova, very flustered, called to the cashier and as Westfall started arguing with Syzmanski she slipped back to the head of the queue, shoved her handbag to the counter above Westfall's open *sparbuch*, and questioned the cashier about her account.

Dispensing with Syzmanski, Westfall turned back to the cashier at the moment Anna Ivanova had deftly withdrawn her handbag. She apologised, the big lens glasses slipped down on her petite nose, he grinned, she smiled self-consciously, she chattered inanely, withdrew off-screen right. Westfall leaned on the counter and chatted with the cashier who had placed his savings book into the computer aperture. The camera panned across the bank, zoomed to a five-second close-up of each client, and focused back on Westfall as he retrieved his savings book, slipped it into the hip pocket of his jeans and strode out of the bank with a farewell imitation-flyrod-cast to the giggling girl clerk.

The screen glared white as the trail end of the film slapped against the projector.

'Cut on the lights.'

We moved our chairs away from Chervenkov's desk.

'So far not bad,' he commented. 'Any of those other bank clients known to be American or Austrian intelligence men?'

'Positive identification from a moving film is unreliable,' Razin argued.

I kept quiet because I knew my prior instructions to Syzmanski.

'Syzmanski?'

'From the film we made individual blow-ups of the other clients in the bank. Nobody in there is on our files as working for the Americans.'

'Are you confident you were not followed? That there were no other Americans from the I Board watching you film Westfall?'

Syzmanski looked at me for reassurance. I nodded.

'We're confident.'

'*Nichevo. Nichevo*. So far, very good,' Chervenkov rasped. 'Now Sergei, I presume all that play acting of your female cinema actress with the handbag was to microfilm Westfall's bank account.'

'We were somewhat worried that we might not intercept his savings book before he retrieved it from the cashier.'

'The microfilm camera was in the handbag?' asked Razin.

'Why yes, it was in the handbag.'

'Well I should say that all this activity and expense have proved nothing,' he complained, scratching his scalp. 'I want to see the photocopies of Westfall's savings book.'

'Syzmanski?'

'They are being reproduced on the printer.'

Chervenkov, Razin and I waited silently for five minutes until Syzmanski returned.

The black-and-white prints were still wet and drooped at the edges. We crowded around Chervenkov's desk. He pulled over a desk lamp and we looked at the figures. There were many computer print-outs and calculations, dates of deposit and withdrawals running back over the past two years, but it was the bottom line we needed and which would justify the entire effort.

'Austrian schillings 676,500.'

'And in dollars?'

I worked it out. 'Depending on the exchange rate, roughly $52,000.'

'What was your original estimate, Sergei?'

'About $47,000.'

'The son of a bitch has been at it longer than we thought. Do those deposit dates check with his I Board visits to Czechoslovakia?'

'Not exactly. There will be a delay of one month or six weeks depending on how quickly he placed the paintings with the Vienna art dealer.'

'But this is what you want?'

'This,' I allowed myself a chilly smile, 'is exactly what I want.'

That wasn't the end of it, of course, because although we now had Westfall's bank figures in our possession it still remained to be decided what we were going to do with them. Chervenkov, unexpectedly, became rather daring. I suppose he was surprised that we had progressed this far in the Westfall operation without major difficulty. He raised the possibility of leaking the allegation of Westfall's embezzlement to the Austrian press. Razin blanched at the suggestion. His counterproposal involved an informal approach to Westfall whereby I would hand over the photocopy of the savings book in return for a vague pledge of American good behaviour.

I commented dryly that, while this undoubtedly would cause much soul-searching among the American intelligence community, it hardly promised returns commensurate with our efforts.

'The point of attack should be Westfall's boss-man, Stillwater.'

'The Texan?'

'He would simply sack Westfall.'

'Not necessarily,' I objected. 'This Stillwater is apparently concerned with maintaining a rather hypocritical pure-as-snow reputation for his congressional overseers. But he needs people like Westfall to perform his dirty work. Threaten him with disclosure and it will damage his carefully cultivated relations with his superiors in Washington. It will also make him fearful of losing Westfall, who so admirably performs tasks Stillwater studiously avoids.'

'And if Stillwater can convince his authorities to abandon attacks on our Soviet officials, we give him the original photographs of Westfall's bank book? If not, they go to the Austrian press. A trade-off.'

'Yes, a trade-off.'

The Tartar-blooded Chervenkov watched me with hard professional eyes. His gaze switched to Razin. He brushed his hand through his thick black hair and took a decision.

'Very well, Sergei. You do it.'

'Go directly to Stillwater, director of the Vienna I Board?'

'Go very directly,' he growled.

Then Chervenkov, the no-nonsense *Rezident*, took us all by surprise. He extracted from his desk a leather pouch containing a half-dozen hand-rolled Havana leaf cigars, exported for special occasions by our fraternal Cuban allies.

'One doesn't want to be too premature with the celebrations, but, it appears in order. You, Razin?'

Razin took a cigar.

'Smoke, Sergei?'

'Very rarely.'

'Well, this is rare enough. Congratulations.'

'Thank you,' I said, taking the cigar.

Syzmanski came in and he got one too. We sat there smiling and smoking Cuban cigars, and somebody brought in vodka and we poured glasses all around. It was eight o'clock in the evening. Another day was ending and Daria's count was nearing eighteen but I was going to terminate the Westfall operation before eighteen days and that, so it appeared, was cause enough to be festive.

Light-headed from lack of sleep, liquor and tobacco, giddy and still exuberant, I had one more task to perform before driving to my residence in the 19th district. This involved the all-night public telex operator at the central post office. Using a very simple code to my south Austrian associates, I directed them to forward their savings books to me for purposes of routine administrative control, or so the telex implied.

In reality I would use one of the *sparbuchs* to withdraw cash for Daria. I had the code word – *butterbrot* – but I needed the *sparbuchs*. I gave myself three to five days for the savings books to arrive, and this would cut our margin to about thirteen days, or less than two weeks before I would be forced to expatriate Daria to Switzerland.

Maybe it was going to be enough, I thought, my head still buzzing from the rich tobacco as I drove through Vienna's evening traffic. Maybe there would be time and we could do it neatly and with style and her removal would be effected professionally with no snarled threads that would trail back in my direction.

Yes, I was certain now that it could be handled with a minimum of damage. A very minimum. I was still convinced as I locked my Lada limousine and walked down the flagstone walkway and saw the single light burning through my residence window.

Training and instinct took control. I never stopped. The saliva rising thick and chalky in my throat, I slammed into the door and hurled down the little hallway determined to meet them head on, in a rush, low to keep the target area down. They . . . who were they? The Americans now that we had shut the trap? Their Austrian lackeys? Viennese police rifling my apartment?

Then I heard it, the low repetitive moan, the stifled wail of something small and afraid and alone. I crashed into the living-room. Rocking forward on her knees, hands clasped protectively to her temples, Daria was slumped on the floor.

I pulled her to her feet, brushed the hair back from her feverish face and shook her until her eyes began to focus.

'Re. . . the telegram. Recalled.'

I sat her on the edge of the desk and held her head in my hands until she began to bring herself under control.

'Just tell me quietly.'

She motioned behind me. I turned. Thrown carelessly on the floor was an Adidas shoulder bag.

'I'm running, Sergei.'

'They recalled him. The Bulgarians summoned your father?'

She nodded. I left her sitting there, found some vodka which I poured into the first kitchen glass available and watched her while she drank it down.

'What time, Daria?'

She stared at me blankly.

'What time is he to be recalled. This week? Today? Tomorrow?'

'I could not find you. The telephone. . .' the sentence broke off. 'He was returned. To Sofia. This morning for consultations. Nice and diplomatic. Balkan airlines, and they were quick and thorough about it.'

'You bolted? The Bulgarians put him on the flight without you?'

'What the hell do you think I did? Waited for them to present me with flowers and bon bons?' The colour had started to return to her face. She waved the glass in my direction, and I poured another dose of vodka. She tossed it down and wiped her mouth with the back of her hand, staring at me sullenly. From her reviving emotions I presumed Daria had returned from the point of collapse.

I walked around and sat behind the desk and covered my face with my hands. My father-in-law . . . the return from Hungary . . . Olga . . . Chervenkov and our entrapment of Westfall . . . it was all beyond my strength. And now Daria was running and had come to ground in my apartment. With the Bulgarian security service undoubtedly less than one hour behind her. The Bulgarians would turn instantly to the Soviets for backup and technical assistance. This meant that in addition to my other difficulties Razin would emerge as my adversary in the search for Daria.

The sap was draining out of me. My body slumped limp and yielding. Hares before hounds, driven into corners, eyes glazed with fear, weak and unmoving.

'Do you have a change of clothes and your passport in the Adidas bag?'

'Yeah. It was all the time I had.'

My mind stirred limply, attempting to remember timetables and calendars. Notice boards and tickets flickered across my vision. It was 10:02. There would be no flights from the Vienna airport to anywhere we wanted to reach. No time to execute my elaborately planned *sparbuch* cash withdrawal. I was too tired to try and drive her in the Lada. That left one method of transportation and it was the slowest but it would have to suffice.

Sluggishly I motioned her to hand me the telephone. Another four minutes bled off the clock before I could get anyone at the Wesbanhof to answer the telephone. Yes, the surly Austrian clerk confirmed, the train with international carriages for Munich and Zurich departs 10:47. After some harsh prodding she confirmed that sleeping compartments were available for reservation. I booked one, all of one.

'Get your bag and your passport and get in the car.'

'You put me on the train for Zurich? Alone, Sergei?'

'No, Daria. Not alone. Sergei has been trained to do things thoroughly.'

'And your embassy? When you do not appear in the morning?'

'If we are fortunate they will assume I am recovering from the after-effects of hangovers and unexpected cigars.'

I took her by the arm and we ran for the car and drove rapidly for the station where the porters were slamming doors and shrilling their whistles and normally I would never have approached the train carriages without putting the complete platform under observation but I had broken all the rules and I might as well break the last of them. The train lurched out of the station. 10:47. The Swiss frontier was all night away.

Chapter 15

The sleeping compartment wasn't as spacious as the Palace of Versailles but it wasn't so bad. There were two bunk beds with sheets tucked back over the Austrian state rail lines woollen blankets, overhead baggage racks we didn't need, mirror, a carafe of mineral water, and fold-down sink with brass nozzles and running water.

I locked the door and pulled down the window shade. Then I sank onto the bottom bunk, jerked open my necktie, pressed my palms to my eyelids and tried to control the muscle stutters that cramped my breathing.

Daria extracted a beauty kit from her Adidas bag, turned on the cold water and began daubing her face with cotton pads and liquid witch hazel astringent. Then she spent the next ten minutes applying her mascara.

The electric-powered locomotive ground slowly through the hills of the Wienerwald. An official rap sounded on the door. I opened it to face the plump, gold-braided sleeping coach conductor who wanted our tickets and reservations.

'*Reisepass*?' I questioned, wanting to know when he would take away the passports for the night.

The official returned the tickets, snuck an appreciative glance at Daria, and in good Viennese dialect told me passports weren't required before Linz on the Danube, an hour and half away. I locked the metal frame door and looked for a chain link but there was no chain link. The bolt lock was all the protection we were going to get.

Daria watched me from the mirror as I slouched back on the bottom bunk.

'Where are the life savings, counsellor? I didn't see you carrying your money belt when we ran from the house.'

'Cash, in my pocket, and there are some travellers' cheques. I didn't exchange them in Hungary.'

'How much, huh?'

'Not as much as there should have been, if you had given me advance notice.'

She swore quietly as she smudged her eyeshadow.

'You got all the advance notice you needed in McDonalds.'

'I do not yet draw Ambassadorial salary.'

'Please don't get smart. Right? How much?'

'About enough to purchase a return aircraft ticket for myself from Zurich to Vienna.'

She spun around.

'What do you mean back to Vienna?'

'Sit down, Daria.'

'Answer the question.'

I was so tired I lapsed into Russian.

'Say it in bloody English!'

'Very well. I shall say it most precisely: we shall cross the Swiss frontier at seven. Arrival Zurich Hauptbahnhof at 8:40. The rail station adjoins the Swissair terminal and I can make a direct connection to Zurich Flughaven for the 10:10 flight to Vienna.'

'I bet you even know the numbers.'

'SR 802 Daria darling.'

'You bastard.'

I let it pass. We were both showing the strain.

'You're dropping me, right? Throwing me to the dogs? What the hell am I supposed to do with myself in Zurich? Stand alone in the rain? Rummage in the garbage cans? A stray cat at the *tierschutz* gets better treatment.'

'I don't think there is much need to continue until you end this hysteria.' I watched the flared nostrils and nasty slant of her eyelids.

'OK, buddy boy, I am no longer hysteric. Tell me what to do.'

'You will register at any Zurich pensione. Fill out the passport form. Take a small room with meals and sit still.'

'I don't want to put my name and passport number on a form the hotel clerk could pass to the Bulgarians.'

'You, not the hotel clerk, fill out the form. In Switzerland they never ask to see your passport. Call yourself Signorina Desdimona or something. Babble a little Italian. Invent a passport number.'

'And where is the great Othello during all this?'

'I fly back to Vienna. That reduces the suspicion in my embassy. Also, I will attempt to check the Bulgarian security officials. As soon as I can withdraw cash, I'll fly back to Zurich.'

'Then with your funds in my pocket I walk into the Swiss ministry of foreign affairs in Bern and ask for asylum. That's the scenario?'

I shrugged.

'Well you're generous as hell. It's going to be thrilling. Sitting in some dumpy hotel waiting for the Bulgarians or the KGB to crash down the door.'

I took the carafe and poured a glass of mineral water which I tried to force down my locked throat. Generosity, I thought bitterly. What is generosity? My throat was constricted. Finally I was able to swallow some of the mineral water. I was throwing away my career for this woman. Generosity.

Lights flickered under the window shade. The train

lost momentum. Cautiously I raised the shade. We were entering the small town of St Pölten fifty kilometres west of Vienna.

I opened the compartment door, stood in the passageway and peered through the window to study the station platforms. Several late-night passengers were boarding the carriages. Postal employees transferred mail sacks to the carriage behind the engine. Local rustics only. I stepped inside, locked the door and finished the glass of mineral water. The engine whistle moaned sadly as the train pulled from the station and headed through rolling hill country towards Linz in the upper Danube valley.

Daria stood with her back to the window. Then she came to me and wrapped her arms around my shoulders and buried her dark head on my shoulder.

'I am so sorry, Sergei.'

I inhaled the scent of citron and dark skin and jasmine perfume in her long black hair. And then in my weariness I saw Ing. Sokolovskiy standing at the embassy window in Budapest, listening to the first sounds of a new summer morning. *Da*, I had said, *da*, I wish always to remain with Olga. Olga with the cool northern grey morning in her eyes, the blonde head and robust bosom and tall strong thighs. Olga who with her Sokolovskiy attachment to a single object had fixed her concentration on a personal intellectual achievement I so poorly understood. Yet this was the same woman who had never abused my generosity. Throughout adversity or success, discouragement or promotion, she had given of herself to advance my career. Was she now saying she wanted her turn? That she had been the buttress of my achievements and now she, with or without my understanding, needed her own accomplishment? With the long tapered brown arms of Daria clasped around my shoulders I began to comprehend what Olga had attempted. It was very intellectual and northern, there was no wine or olive oils and figs or Bulgarian tobaccos in Thracian sunshine, it was balsam and pine and snow blowing crystalline on December mornings, but what Olga had done was logical and consistent. My body stirred as Daria pressed against me but my senses were rekindled for the woman far away in Russia, not the warm-skinned Bulgarian girl who embraced me.

The metal door rang with a sharp rap. We must have journeyed a quarter of the distance from St Pölten to Linz. This would be the conductor demanding our passports. Daria sat on the bunk with her back to the window as I turned to the door and called out for the conductor to identify himself.

'*Gutn amnd, gemsma die Reisepässe*!' the man bellowed in thick Vienna dialect. Satisfied, I relaxed, reached down, turned the bolt and opened the door.

There was one individual out there but not the one I expected.

'Ciao, you all! Mind if I drop in?' drawled Westfall with a big grin on his face.

I reacted instinctively without thought control. I grabbed Westfall by the collar, dragged him into the compartment, shot the bolt and slammed his back against the metal door. Turning my thigh so he could not knee me in the groin, I slapped his hands apart, drew back my right hand with second joint knuckles locked into a striking blade, kept the weight on the balls of my feet, and with my free left hand slapped his underarms to find a weapon. He was unarmed. My eyesight had narrowed to two yellow dots. I stood back, breathing tightly, ready to slash him across the throat if he lunged at me, and watched him as he stood there in his jeans, cowboy boots and beige shooting jacket, grinning in immense enjoyment.

'All that frisking isn't really necessary in the presence of a lady,' he laughed, raising his hand to stroke his clipped RAF moustache.

I glanced back at Daria.

Very quietly from the interior of her Adidas shoulder bag she had removed what looked like a Smith & Wesson .32 hammerless revolver, which she was pointing directly at my midsection.

'Sit down, Sergei,' Daria whispered. 'It's time the three of us had a little conversation.'

Chapter 16

'I think the first thing to do,' Westfall was standing with his back to the sink and mirror, 'is to give you a drink of water. You look all done in.'

'I am surprised you do not instantly produce a flask of American Jim Beam whisky. Stop all the posing and state your terms. Did you give her that thing?' nodding towards Daria's revolver.

'Uh, yeah.'

'You realise, Daria,' I continued, fighting against the rage of tears that nearly blocked my vision, 'your career is more promising in front of the cameras than behind them. That was marvellous character acting.'

'Please don't be sarcastic. This is not a particularly pleasant moment.'

'What about our little conjugal life in the apartment?'

'Very enjoyable.' She tossed her head. 'You're pretty good. I did what I had to do.'

'Shall we inform Mr Westfall of the proper declension of the noun whore in Russian and Bulgarian?'

'Now now, no domestic tiffs,' Westfall intervened. 'First things first. Give me your passport in case the conductor shows up.'

'Just keep the safety on that revolver,' I told Daria as I handed Westfall my passport.

'She'll keep it on as long as I tell her to keep it on.'

'So you've been orchestrating Daria, helpless refugee in search of asylum?'

'She is in search of asylum, and it is my duty to see that she achieves it. You want to listen to the rest of it?'

'Shouldn't you shake me out first? I could be carrying dangerous and menacing weapons?'

Westfall shook his head.

'It has already been verified you have no pistol holster,' Daria commented dryly. 'I regret if you thought my arms around your shoulders were nothing more than a final embrace.'

Without answering I reached for the hand towel by the sink and covered my face as the tears of rage and betrayal brimmed over my eyelids. My shoulders rocked with convulsions. The two of them watched silently as I sat there wringing the salt dregs of my total defeat.

A great deal of time elapsed before I could face them.

'Very well, Westfall,' I said softly. 'Tell me the rest of it. What do you want from me?'

'Now, the first element to consider is this train, its destination, and who's on it. As you undoubtedly know, we are scheduled to cross the Austrian–Swiss frontier at 7:00am. "We" is Daria and me. You no longer have your passport. I have taken it from you. Therefore, at the latest, you will be compelled by the frontier police to exit the train carriage on Austrian soil before the train crosses into Switzerland.'

Westfall still drawled with his horrible provincial American accent. But it occurred to me that he was speaking with considerably more precision than I had previously noticed.

'Congratulations, Daria,' I commented. 'I presume you will not simply reside in Zurich? On to ski at St Moritz?'

'Can we stop fussing and let me continue?' Westfall

interjected. 'Good. Now, through my embassy the Swiss authorities have been notified, and will accept, Daria's request for legal asylum. In view of the Bulgarian security force's past record ample police protection will be assured. . .'

I judged the distance separating Daria from me. She held the revolver with considerable competence. Despite the rattle and sway of the carriage the dark bore of the muzzle didn't waver two centimetres off its axis. From the four visible chambers, I could see the dull copper shine of the .32 magnum cartridges. At this range one of those slugs would rip a hole through my chest the size of a horse's hoof. I looked back at Westfall.

'It is important for you to know, Sergei, that representatives of the Bulgarian security service and the Soviet KGB are seated in the carriages connected to both ends of this sleeping wagon. They are there because I telephoned your embassy in Vienna and indicated that you and Daria had a reservation on this carriage.'

That hit me as though Daria had pulled the trigger. I stared at the American in complete disbelief. Until this moment I had struggled with the knowledge of Daria's betrayal but clung to the strand of hope that I could return to Vienna undetected by Razin's counterintelligence operatives.

'Ever heard of a, uh, Mr Razin?'

'He is our embassy chief of security.'

'Well, he has conveniently come along for the ride. He's up front in the next carriage. When you get off the train, wherever, whatever station platform, Linz, Salzburg, Innsbruck, the frontier, I have this real funny feeling that you are going to have a great deal of unpleasant company.'

'Why are you doing this to me?' I shouted. 'What

do you want from me you son of a whore!'

'Come on now. Yelling will get you nowhere.' He paused while I bowed my head, humiliated, struggling in the snares which entrapped me. 'There is a little option. Like this: I give you your passport back. You stay on the train. The three of us breeze into Switzerland. And you and Daria waltz into asylum together.'

'That would be defection.'

'Why now, it would indeed! Sergei would become a defector!'

'Listen to him, Sergei. It will be terrible for you if you surrender to Razin.'

'You are giving me a choice?'

'Call it what you want to call it. Get off the train and rush into the waiting arms of the KGB. Or go through to Switzerland and declare yourself a refugee from the Soviet government. You should believe me,' he smiled innocently, a good ole country boy, 'you have absolutely no other alternative.'

'In Switzerland,' I said haltingly, 'your organisation would want me?'

'Well, I guess, eventually. Just a friendly chat. To compare notes, talk shop, that sort of thing. I would guess that it would be considerably, ah, less mentally *demanding*,' he shrugged for emphasis, 'less trying, than a debriefing at the hands of your old comrade, Razin.'

'Please Sergei. Don't you see it as your only choice?'

The carafe was empty. I placed a glass under the nozzle and drank the *non-potable* water like a whipped dog.

'Why. Why?' I spat out weakly.

'Why what?'

'Why am I being persecuted by you? What have I done to you? Why did you use Daria against me?

What is it that you want of me?'

'To answer your questions you must realise that, like most things in this world, this case has an economic base. Very Hegelian. Very Marxist.'

'I am totally uninvolved in economic decision making.'

'Why so you are! But, tough break, you are deeply involved with an individual who makes very big economic decisions. Decisions which, unfortunately have not found favour with my masters and my regime.'

The carafe rattled emptily in the rack as the train clacked across the steel rails. Against the roll and pitch of the carriage dim lights streaked by in the night. I was slipping into a haze of depression and weariness and was barely capable of following Westfall's monologue.

'No guesses?'

'I cannot understand you, Westfall. You have lost all reason.'

'Ever hear of an old chap called Ing. G. V. Sokolovskiy, Minister of Petroleum and Mining, Union of Soviet Socialist Republics? Member, Central Committee, Communist Party of the Soviet Union? Any of that ring a bell?'

'Olga's father. My father-in-law.'

'Correct. Now, some time ago, Ing. Sokolovskiy, Olga's daddy, had to choose between two competing consortia for off-shore oil drilling technology. Unfortunately, one of the groups represented our good ole allies in Great Britain.'

'And British Petroleum won the deal. Partial payment in 10 million tons of petroleum annually at a seven per cent price cut.'

'You are not as uninformed as you pretend.'

He rocked back in his cowboy boots and brushed a

lock of dark hair from his forehead. Had the Americans mounted this operation against my father-in-law? I thought quickly. Had they used Daria to entrap me in some wild attempt to pressure the Soviet petroleum ministry?

'The American oil group's demand was not so exorbitant,' he was saying. 'A 25 million ton concession with a ten per cent price reduction. But the Brits scrounged for the deal. If they had held out on our terms we could have given them a nice slice of the action.'

'You are mad if you think the Soviet ministry can be so intimidated that it will reverse its decision! My father-in-law would be dismissed if he now cancelled the British agreement!'

'Why, we don't reckon he would cancel the deal, that is, this deal,' Westfall drawled. 'It's all over an' done with, sad to say. But we do want his ministry to be a little more considerate the next time around. I say, "his ministry", because when news of your little peccadilloes reaches Moscow he may get the chop. You are going to smear anybody who has ever gotten near you.'

'You overestimate my importance. You have no concept of the Soviet system. Mass family responsibility for the fault of one member ended with Stalin.'

'That's news to me,' Westfall laughed. 'Let's see: Ing. Sokolovskiy's son-in-law has, one, committed adultery while his daughter was back home in Moscow. Two, assisted a Bulgarian ambassador's daughter to defect to the West . . . Three, failed to inform the KGB or the Bulgarians of this little train trip to Switzerland. Four, may, if he so chooses, defect to Switzerland on his own account. Shall I go on? Shouldn't we add a real or attempted embezzlement of KGB cash? That'd be a beauty. Go down great with headquarters.'

I had risen to my feet in anger but now, slowly, like a bellows under pressure, crumpled and slid back to the bunk. He could crush me, I thought desperately. He could place intolerable pressure on my family. If I was apprehended by Razin my behaviour could be utilised to ruin Olga's father. But if I defected to the Swiss my entire family's safety would be in jeopardy. Through the glint of salt-stung eyes I tried to grapple with the thought of Olga expelled from the university, Ing. Sokolovskiy driven from his ministry and the Central Committee. A tribunal. A prison sentence. Was Westfall correct? Had I only two alternatives? Surrender to Razin at the Swiss frontier? Or defection? Had I a third choice? If I did not defect, but was not captured by my service? If I could return of my own free will? Was it the only way remaining to reduce the penalty for my family, if not for me or the ruin of my career?

'The point, Sergei, is that Soviet petroleum is rather valued in capitalist refineries. We like it. Particularly if we can do a deal and get it cheap. As long as the price is right, we see no reason why you Russians should be selling it to the British and not to us.'

He bent his lanky frame, glanced out the window as the train streaked past a silent farm village, then slouched against the sink. 'Thus this Sergei–Olga–Daria episode, and its most regrettable ruin for the Soviet Minister of Mines and Petroleum, should serve as a little lesson. We like to play clean, and if you boys play clean, then so can we. But if you Soviets continue to deny us commercial concessions for a strategic commodity merely because a competitor has made a more attractive offer, then we are prepared now, and in the future, to play very very dirty.'

'You are a disgrace to the United States of America! You do not serve the American people! You are a hireling of the monopolistic corporations that exploit them!'

'Don't ask me, mate. I just work here.'

'Was that your I Board organisation attacking Soviet embassy personnel throughout Europe?'

'My organisation took no direct part. But there is a standing agreement with other American agencies, where possible, to stir things up. Anyway, I've been rather busy with your case. Took one he-ell of a time to set you up.'

Keeping her trigger finger very steady Daria leaned across and mopped the sweat from my temples. My tongue was swollen with thirst. I glanced at her dully before turning to Westfall.

'What was that charade in Czechoslovakia? The Austerlitz battlefield? Your impressive purchases? Jan Siska's paintings? The sales at the Vienna art merchants? Your profitable bank account?'

'As somebody said, by misdirection we find direction out.'

'Don't quote books at me, you lackey!'

'Sit down, Sergei.'

'The lady is very good with the gun. Take your paws off me and sit down.'

My chest rocking with anger, glaring at Daria, I released his shirt collar and dropped to the bunk.

'Do you know what the Czech police would have done to that old man, Jan Siska?'

'It's all rather standard,' Westfall ignored my question as he slipped into a misplaced British intonation. 'We . . . Stillwater my director and I . . . we constructed an operational plan and a deception plan. The operational plan was to deceive and punish one member of Petroleum Minister Sokolovskiy's family.

We had certain ideas for your wife, whom I happen to find a very attractive lady.' He bowed and clicked his boot heels. 'But Olga proved most chaste and upright and difficult to approach. Involved in her thesis. We had some reserve ploys for you that involved money. Then there was Daria.'

'Yes, Daria. Most delightful,' I spat at them. 'And I am certain she repaid you lavishly with her erotic favours.'

'No. Incorrect. Sorry to disappoint you. I run an ethical operation.'

'Don't be vulgar and stupid, Sergei. If you wish to know, I was introduced to Westfall by some students in Germany. I made it clear I had no intention of going back to Bulgaria. But I needed help. He arranged asylum and cash to support me, provided I would cooperate with him in Vienna.'

Not knowing if I would ever see her again, I turned to face her dark eyes, bronzed skin, hair tousled wildly across her shoulders.

'I cannot pretend that I regret my actions,' she said softly. 'But if it is of any consolation to you, I want you to know that our time together was very pleasant for me.' And for three seconds she knotted my stomach the way she had always done, from the Bulgarian embassy reception to kisses in the rain by the Danube to sweat-streaked nights in the bed where Olga had once slept.

'You must have had a low opinion of my resistance,' I said hoarsely to Westfall. 'But you could not have predicted that I would behave with complete irresponsibility?'

'As I said, we had several contingency plans. The appearance of Daria at the Bulgarian cocktail reception was just one on the list. But after she described your behaviour, we put the other plans back in the filing cabinet.'

'What was that at the heuriger? You and Stillwater showing up when Daria and I were drinking wine?'

'Wanted to rattle you a little. Shake you up. Divert your concentration. Very standard operational technique. So when you went down to get your plate of pickles and sausage, Daria slipped out to a telephone booth and called Stillwater.'

'But she did not telephone you to warn that I would take this train tonight?'

'It was pretty well programmed. I instructed her to reach your apartment with her mock derangement and simulated flight after 8:00pm. This would be too late to make suitable connections if you ran for the airport. I calculated it would be too dangerous for you to drive to Switzerland. That left the one international train we are now on.'

'What the hell do you mean Daria's simulated flight?'

'Among a string of other failures, you didn't do much checking.'

'Daddy is still in Vienna.'

'There was no recall of Ambassador Kaladzhiev,' Westfall grinned, brushing his clipped moustache. 'He was not placed on a flight to Sofia. He remains in his function in Vienna. We realised, of course, that you would not risk exposure by asking too many questions around the Bulgarian embassy. But we had to allege the ambassador's recall and Daria's woe to establish a reason for bolting to Switzerland.'

'You still have not answered my questions about Czechoslovakia. Exposing that man Siska. Your bank account of schillings 676,500.'

'That was the deception plan. A counterpoint to our operational objectives. There was always the chance that your earlier training would prevail and you would scrutinise Daria's role with more scepticism than you actually demonstrated. We figured if you believed you were leading me into a trap you would overlook the one into which you had blundered.'

'Will you keep all that money you were making? A big profit. Very businesslike.'

'So sorry. The working capital came from authorised I Board funds. The profits will be returned to Stillwater's account. But I must say,' he yawned, 'your Czech secret police allies are pretty dim-witted. We had to coat-tail and drag scent all over the ground before somebody sat up and took notice. At least I had an enjoyable rugby match up there. We defeated Lokomotiva Brno 21–12.'

'The Czech police bastards owe me a case of Pilsner beer. They never paid up,' I said gloomily, preyed upon by evidence of the careful detail by which Westfall had cast his web around me. And strangely, deep inside my weariness, I noted my spark of professional admiration for his enormous attention to detail. His masquerade in Czechoslovakia had completely camouflaged his plan to entrap me.

'For instructional purposes,' he grinned, 'please note your other slip-ups: fish odour from one of your sardine-eating technicians stinking up my apartment to warn me it had been ransacked. And the bit in the bank with the cute little girl ahead of me with the mini-camera in her handbag. I fell out of the cradle learning that one.'

To defect in Switzerland, secure personal safety but ruin my family, I thought feverishly. Or be taken by Razin, returned to Moscow under arrest, and be utilised to discredit my father-in-law. Alternatives? Was there no further choice? I felt the last reserve of my strength turn to water. The train whistle moaned like a demented soul across the night. The beautiful

Daria wavered into a witch's mask before my fading vision. Westfall's grin and slashed cheekbone rippled into a death's skull as final weariness settled over my consciousness.

'Westfall, you have done well,' I said. 'But you have acted with greater competence than required. Why? Why have you pursued me thus?'

He watched me very calmly. Benign. Not without sympathy, now that he had ruined my life.

'We spoke of this once, sitting by the Imperial Hotel on the ring in Vienna,' he answered quietly. 'American officials and the policy they create are portrayed as impulsive, uncontrolled, unsophisticated, emotional and ill-disciplined. But the Russians are logical, chill, selective, masters of the set-piece game of chess.'

'You turned this case into a personal vendetta.'

'Well, yes, sort of. You see, Sergei, I personally grew rather tired of hearing how we were so inefficient and bumbling, while you Russians were the masters of spycraft. In reality the labels and tags are meaningless. I as an American could act, I believe, with empirical objectivity. You the Russian could fall prey to the most basic excesses of lust and emotion.'

Muscles of water, I thought. Strength seeping from my body. The third alternative. Had I strength to fight for the one chance that could keep my wife and her father from destruction?

'Agree, Sergei?'

I rose unsteadily, watching with fear as Daria raised the axis of the revolver muzzle to focus on my chest. The hurtling train shrieked on its tracks. Dull copper cartridges glinted in their chambers.

'Agree?'

'Yes, Wes, I agree. An excess of lust and emotion . . .'

I uncoiled with all the strength left in my body. My hand shot upward to the red metal handle anchored above the door. The *notbremse*, emergency brake. I yanked downward, stripping the restraining lead safety cable. It was the oldest gambit in our textbook, but, then, none of my methods had been particularly innovative. The engine howled as its brakes locked automatically, buckling the carriages, hurling us to the floor. The lights of the compartment flickered and died with a short circuit. I struggled to my feet, ripped the empty water carafe from its rack, and hurled it into the compartment window. The glass shattered into a hundred jagged fragments. Daria was trying to crawl back to the bunk. Westfall grappled at my feet. With one last effort I hurled myself through the broken window as the train ground to a halt with showers of sparks on the steel rails. I hit the gravel embankment, knocked the breath from my lungs, and rolled into a drainage ditch. I lay there gasping for breath, rose to my knees, and staggered away from the train. Electric torches shone along the embankment. Men were running in the darkness. I clambered over a wire fence, struggled across a muddy ploughed field. A man bellowed in Russian. Three other men were running behind him. Exhausted, I sank to both knees and crawled into a concrete culvert. I wanted to go north towards the Danube. I had broken through the window and fallen on the south side of the train. As the English might say, I was on the wrong side of the tracks.

Chapter 17

My escape appeared to have been terminated before it had truly begun. I had crawled into a trap. The far end of the concrete culvert was blocked with brush, debris and mud. Men were following my path across the field. Distinct and clear in the night air, I could hear them calling one to another in Russian. I squirmed forward in the silt which coated the bottom of the culvert. Electric torch lights flickered across the oval entrance. Please God, I muttered wearily, please God allow me not to fall into the hands of these men who will destroy my family, but there was no god listening or the one who did was unimpressed with foxhole incantations.

'*Sledy*!' They had found my tracks.

'*Bistryeye*! *Bistryeye*!'

'*Suda*! *Svet*!' A man was standing above me on the roof of the culvert. He swung an electric torch beam to focus inside the passage. Eyes dilated in fear, I pressed into the darkness at the back of the culvert. The arc of light crept towards me, hesitated, wavered, inched forward, I clawed against the mud blocking the escape from the culvert, the light crawled toward me, halted, extinguished. Blackness.

'*Nikovo nyet*! *Ubyezhal*.' Nothing. They had not seen me in the darkness.

I heard them running away down a gravel road. My stomach reeled as I clamped my teeth to fight against sickness. I inched forward to the opening of the culvert and drew in great draughts of fresh air. Then, like a wave of dark sea enveloping a drowning man, a mantle of weariness wrapped around me and I slept face down in the mud.

The chill of the dawn woke me at 5:00am. Cautiously I raised my head above the culvert and looked across the misty hills. There were no trackers to be seen beating the fields of corn for my hiding place. The sense of personal quiet and safety was as all-pervading as it was treacherous. I knew I had won nothing more than a reprieve. Razin and his men would throw out a screen to snare me. Or if the police apprehended me I would be forced to declare my diplomatic status and would be delivered to the clutches of my embassy's security force.

I had no cover story. There was simply nothing I could concoct to explain my muddy presence, sitting in a culvert beside an Austrian cornfield. It was hopeless enough to be comic and ridiculous. Arrest by local constables, who would take me for a vagrant or madman, seemed only minutes away. A reasonable amount of pocket cash and a reserve of travellers' cheques appeared the sole consolation of my position.

Against this hopeless outlook my objective was to reach a neighbouring socialist country, surrender of my own free will, and request repatriation to my superiors in Moscow. I could then document the Americans' subversion against me. A voluntary return held the slim hope of clemency for Olga and her father. But if I was seized and returned by Razin he would present me as a defector for whom no mercy was justified. Razin had personal reasons for wanting to capture me. My successful evasion would wreck his career chances of ever serving again as an embassy security officer outside the Soviet Union.

It was out of the question to return to Vienna. The

Hungarian border to the east was far too distant. It would be necessary to cross the Danube and head north toward Czechoslovakia. That posed its own problems. I had no passport and could not cross into the Czech lands at any normal frontier post. The great length of the frontier was sealed off by barbed wire, ploughed strips and minefields. I needed to find a point where the wire had been pulled back from the frontier so that I could reach a Czech border patrol in a buffer zone. This would be possible on a river line. One of the smaller rivers in northern Austria. I struggled to recall the maps of the Austrian-Czech border at which I had glanced during my previous automobile journey to Czechoslovakia. The Thaya river meandered along the border south of Brno. This could be waded, chest-deep. I would need to reach one of the Austrian villages on the Thaya. Laa or Hardegg. At what distance? I must have jumped from the train after passing Melk or Ybbs. On a direct line, as the crow flies to the north east, this would be a journey of a hundred kilometres. Double that figure across winding hill roads.

This distance could not be walked. The slow postal bus system would be less difficult than auto-stopping, but any bus driver would alert the militia as soon as I appeared in my mud-caked suit. Razin and the Austrian police would be searching for a dishevelled Russian refugee. I smiled grimly. I required instant transfiguration into a loden-coated, yodelling, polka-dancing Austrian if there were to be any odds for my survival.

I also realised that it was insane to think of arriving in Moscow, thousands of kilometres away, or even crossing the Czech border, before I reached the town of Ybbs on the Danube, ten kilometres down the road. If I failed to make the first checkpoint, or any of those in between, there would be little need to consider the final objective.

I crawled from the culvert, found a fresh flowing brook where I washed the mud from jacket and trousers, located a direction marker, and began to trudge towards Ybbs. I felt as conspicuous as the Grand Duke Nicholas walking down that farm road. Once I reached the traffic of the Danube market town my nerves began to steady. I merged into the crowd, entered a clothing store, and bought out the stock of Austrian national costumes. Red and white checkered cotton shirt, loden jacket, white loden walking hat, loden knee breeches, red wool knee stockings, and heavy-treaded Koflach hiking boots. I paid straight from the pocket. That cut my cash reserve by fifty per cent but I didn't want to leave a trail of travellers' cheques.

At an apothecary's shop I bought one Bic throw-away razor. Next stop, the municipal *hallenbad*, that glistening glass and ceramic complex of swimming pool, showers and sauna built in every respectable Austrian city. I purchased an entrance ticket, took a locker, stripped, showered, shaved off my grimy beard but left the incipient moustache which had sprouted on my upper lip, parted my hair down the centre like a rustic, and bedecked myself in my man-of-the-mountains hiking outfit.

Hanging abandoned in the locker was my once-exclusive Heinz Mohr suit from Vienna's most distinguished tailor. Mudstained, lacerated. Like my career, ambition, and ethics.

I strode from the locker room, turned into the main hallway for the exit with the intention of walking to the postal bus station. Light streamed through the brick glass at the entrance. Two figures rose from benches beside the cashier's box. Their faces were in darkness and their bodies were silhouetted against the dazzling light diffused through the glass, but the baggy trousers and scuffed shoes read like labels, Made in Moscow.

Fear wriggled in my stomach. Razin's men had followed me to the hallenbad. I had been run to ground.

'*Stoy*!' one of the Russians yelled.

I whirled around, clonked back down the corridor in my hiking boots, wrenched open the steel door leading to the heating plant and pump room, and shot the bolt behind me. I opened the connecting metal fire door and stepped down the concrete steps into the pumping station. Two attendants were eating bread and sausage on a wooden table. They stared at me with curiosity.

'*Von dem sicherheitsrat*!' I stated. All Austrians pay homage to anyone claiming the authority of an inspector. The men stood up from the table.

'*Ausgang*!' I barked, asking for the exit. They motioned to another steel door adjacent to the main filter pumps. Behind me the Russians were striking the locked door with a metal object. I nodded to the attendants, threw open the door and found myself facing a small-town-version shopping centre across an asphalt parking lot.

Walk don't run.

I was half way across when a white Mercedes swerved around the corner of the hallenbad. I bolted for the entrance to the shopping complex. The place was jammed with rural ladies unaccustomed to the intricacies of handling metal shopping push carts. I crashed into one woman carrying a half-dozen boxes of soap powder, tangled with a citified matron who was leading a dachshund on a leash down the toothpaste and deodorant aisle, but I saw that if I could keep moving I could exit through an American-style automatic glass door on the opposite side of the building. It was all out of place in bucolic Austria but I wasn't there to criticise the architecture.

I went right through to the taxi that was waiting on the far side of the building. The driver reluctantly folded his copy of *Sexy* and looked bored with my proposal.

'*Wohin*?' Where to?

'*Zwettl*!' I yelled the first town in northern Austria that I could remember.

The man returned to his reading material and muttered he was allowed by regulations to drive no further than Melk, down the Danube.

I wrenched around. Through the glass of the shopping building I could see two men forcing their way past the push carts.

I laid a 1,000 schilling note on the seat and said 'drive to Melk.'

We pulled from the parking lot as the two men ran through the automatic doors. One of them made the mistake of pushing back through the crowd to the waiting white Mercedes. It would have gone faster had he sprinted around the building. It took some coaxing, but I convinced my driver to use the autobahn to Melk but he didn't break any speed records reaching it.

He wanted to know where in Melk and I told him the ship landing on the Danube. He dropped me beside the ticket office but I wasn't purchasing any tickets for a scenic river cruise downstream to old Vienna. Sweating now in my woollens, I raced up the cobbled streets of Melk away from the river and ran for the postal bus parking area. I jumped the diesel bus for the town of Horn as it lurched from the station.

We crossed the bridge over the Danube below the great Melk monastery, and for the next interminable four hours ground gears up through the broken, forested hill-country north of the Danube. Predictably for sunny tourist-happy Austria the sky went dull, the ceiling closed and a monotonous drizzle began to fall. It was two in the afternoon when we reached the hill town of Horn and across the great expanses of beech forest gloom was descending like it was January.

There was one local girl clerk in the post office. I asked how I could reach the Czech frontier by bus.

'You cannot reach it because the bus is not allowed to pass over the frontier,' she looked at me helpfully through the glass partition of the post-office window. 'For the hiking, it is unpleasant vacation in this weather. Up here it rains for days,' she added, nodding at my loden jacket.

My costume had proved convincing. Congratulations were in order. I was still far removed from the frontier and Razin's men were behind me, the drizzle enveloped the hills, but I had been taken for a dedicated naturalist.

'How near the frontier do you wish?' she asked.

'Excuse me?'

'The bus cannot reach Czechoslovakia, but it can take you to a road junction from where you can walk to Hardegg on the Thaya river,' she explained. 'That is the state boundary. It is good for hiking along the river if you wait until the rains cease.'

I bought a fare. Hunger was gnawing like a fox in my belly. The bus was due in a quarter hour. At a sleepy *gasthaus* I bought a bottle of beer and a greasy sausage, which I bolted down my throat, and ran back to the bus.

We rattled and bumped for another hour, then I left

the bus at a crossroad and headed down a gravel road past fields of wheat and barley in the direction of Hardegg on the river line. The hills were clouded with mist. Daylight was fading. Ahead in the rain I could see the trace of a great cleft, the steep ridges of limestone and shale where the river Thaya had sliced through the hill country along the Czech border. I pulled my wool collar against the rain and trudged down the road, confident now that I could reach the shelter of the conifer forest in the river valley and across the river before darkness. What hit me hit me like I had been clipped from behind by a speed skater. My legs jacked from under me and I landed heavily on my hip.

Only then did the flat crack of the high velocity rifle echo dully across the hill.

Stunned, I attempted to roll on my stomach. My right leg was paralysed. Groggy, eyes narrowed from the shock, I looked up the road. A white Mercedes was parked at the crossroads and a figure was leaning across the hood, steadying a hunting rifle with telescopic sight.

Crack! Chips of limestone stung my forehead as another high-velocity shell ricocheted off the roadway. Numbed from panic, I crawled for the ditch along the edge of the barley field. That shielded me from the line of sight of the Mercedes at the top of the hill, but they would come after me. They would take me crippled and bleeding in the ditch by the roadway. I grasped my right leg, looking for pulp and splintered bone. But the bone was sound. Then I saw that the heel of my hiking boot had been cleaved in half. I had been shot through the lower heel. The heavy boot had deflected the full force of the projectile. I could feel blood soaking into the bottom of my boot. But I could walk if I kept weight on my other leg. Why shoot low?

Whoever had hit me in the heel in that dim light was very, very professional. He was using light ammunition, .27 calibre high velocity. Why had he not sighted down his crosshair and shot me through the skull? Because Razin did not want to kill me. He needed to return me to the KGB living, if crippled.

I wiped my hand across my eyes and looked down the roadway. There were three hundred metres along the barley field to the conifer forest. Then the steep drop down to the river. Across the river was the frontier. Razin's men would not follow me guns blazing into the arms of a Czech border patrol. And I would no longer give them such a facile stand-up target.

Crouching below the level of the grain field I limped down the ditch toward the tree line. The men at the Mercedes were waiting for me to expose myself in the road. Hunching over, virtually crawling on hands and knees, I slowly made my way toward the cover of the conifer forest.

Then the engine of the Mercedes roared with life. Radial tyres squealed on the gravel. They were coming after me. I crawled into the barley, smoothed the uncut grain behind me to conceal my burrow, and watched as the heavy car roared past. They were driving too fast for me to recognise all the occupants but I could detect the bare white skull of Razin beside the driver.

They cut their speed, searching for my tracks and blood spoor, and followed the road which curved down the slope to the village of Hardegg on the river. I bolted diagonally across the grain field and reached the forest. The hill fell away sharply. I could hear the roar of the river below. In the darkness and rain I began to work my way down the steep slope to the Thaya river.

Lights flashed in the forest. Razin had realised he had driven past me, now he and his men had spread out and were trying to comb the slope above the river. I heard them stumbling and cursing. The beam of heavy electric torches pierced through the gloom, casting grotesque human shadows against the conifers. The roar of the river Thaya boiled below as I slid down the ridge. This was allegedly a calm flowing river of moderate depth, but now it rushed through the limestone valley churned with debris and foam. The stream was swollen by the summer rains. Limping, burdened by heavy woollen clothing, could I swim the current to the far river bank?

'*Vot*! *Sledy* . . . *k reke*!' a man bellowed above me on the ridge. They had found the point where I had slid through the leaves and mud.

Torch-beams swung across the ridge, searching for me through the rain. Stones clattered down the limestone cliff. Against the roar of the maddened river I heard Razin's high-pitched voice calling the other trackers.

I stumbled to the river bank, waded into the stream and gasped from shock at the slash of the cold water.

'*Sergei*, *stoyte*!' Razin saw me. Lights pinned me against the swirling river. There was no time to strip my heavy boots or thick woollens. I could stand there and surrender to my oppressors or I could wait, spitted in the blinding electric torches, to be shot through my limbs and crippled and captured or I could hurl myself into the river. I dived forward into the water, struggling against the iced fingers that grasped my legs and drew me downward into freezing green blackness, water poured into my lungs and all was cold blackness as my body was washed out to mid-current and red points burned in my eyes as my head broke once from the surface of the water and I could see Razin shining his torches across the river and then I was again pulled under as my sodden woollen clothing overcame all my strength. Lungs near rupture from the pain, I thrashed from my shoulders, flailed with my arms against the current and held myself above surface long enough to turn my body against the current and struggle towards the far bank.

Ahead I saw three men waving and shouting in a foreign language. They linked arms and struggled into the water. At the end of my strength I made one final lunge in their direction and felt a burly arm catch under my shoulder as I sank beneath the river. Struggling for oxygen, ears drumming from pain, I was drawn from the river and pulled through the tangled willow bushes along the river bank. The men watched me for a very long time as I retched the water from my lungs.

'Czech? Militia?' I asked weakly, looking at their wet brown uniforms and pistol belts.

They nodded.

I said I was Soviet. Notify my embassy in Prague, put me in an automobile, drive to Brno and fly me to Prague, I told them.

You are an official? they questioned.

I looked back across the river at the distant lights sweeping the surface of the water, I looked back at the river bank in the darkness and rain that was Austria and the West and knew I had survived and I said, yes, I am a Soviet official.

Chapter 18

Moscow. Summer had ended and the sky hung heavy with slate-grey clouds. Rain stripped the leaves from the trees, the drains clogged on the asphalt streets and washing hung limply from apartment balconies. I stood at my window and watched the endless block of apartment buildings, old though they were yet new, with cracked masonry and sagging brick, a horizon of grey concrete.

Far below my apartment window blue sparks flashed from the trolley wires. At the trolley stations long queues of office workers huddled wet and cold in the autumn wind. Automobile traffic snaked down the boulevard towards central Moscow. Headlights glowed orange through the exhaust fumes. The rain fell steadily on the pavement, coating windshields with dirty film. The apartment's communal vegetable gardens were overrun with weeds, cucumber vines had turned brown and blackened tomato stalks clung to decayed sticks.

This was my fifth week in detention. The entire apartment building was owned by the KGB and served as domicile for officers whose overseas activity was under inspection. The Lubyanka prison on Dzerzhinsky Square is still utilised to incarcerate delinquents and malcontents, but I had not been housed there. Instead I was sequestered in this concrete flat. And lucky was he who did here abide! My rooms had a WC and shower, a gas ring, a fold-down bed which served also as a divan, writing desk of thin veneer and bureau drawers in which my new clothing was neatly folded. Space indeed, bountiful space beyond the grasp of most Muscovite households.

In my grey synthetic fibre trousers and open-necked white shirt I stood at the window and looked at the rain and recalled when they had first brought me here. I had been flown in from Prague, examined at a clinic, subjected to light surgery on my heel with local anaesthetic, shot full of anti-biotics, barbered and measured for new clothing. Then a black Lada sedan drove to the apartment block where I was checked through glass doors with electric lock apparatus, put into the elevator and shown into my lodgings. And here I rested for a week, sleeping eleven hours daily, cooking omelette and boiled eggs on the gas ring and reading outdated copies of *Sovetsky Sport*. Only then did the interrogations commence. The delay had been due, I reasoned, to the fact that the KGB judicial section required witnesses from Vienna. Thus when my preliminary dispositions began I acted from the assumption that Razin and other Vienna embassy officials had painted my deportment in the blackest of hues.

Western commentators shriek about 3:00am interrogations and knocks on doors. This was not my personal experience. Each day I was driven from the apartment to a featureless stucco building in the Moscow suburbs where I suffered nothing more serious than hip cramp from long hours sitting on wooden chairs, facing a judicial officer behind a desk.

I say 'a' judicial officer, since the examining officials changed frequently. There was none of this distorted fiction about the accused dealing with a single case-officer-interrogator in whom he develops a psychological bond of dependence. No. No. My inquisitors were all rather bland KGB bureaucrats with spectacles and dandruff and other human frailties who rotated frequently once they had recorded a particular set of dispositions. There was no apparent pattern to the questioning, much of it seemed unimaginative or marginal, and this proved unnerving:

'What was your intention regarding the Bulgarian embassy in Vienna?'

'They invited me to cocktail parties,' I shrugged.

Or, 'At what point in your career did you establish the fact that the American Joint Intelligence Operations Board was located across the Key Bridge of Washington?'

Or, 'Is it coincidental that your estimate of the American, Westfall's, earnings were significantly below the actual total?'

'On your own initiative did you appear at the Vienna University?'

I said it was Daria's idea. Why avoid it?

'To what extent did Miss Kaladzhiev question the nature of your employment in the Soviet Vienna embassy?'

'At any time did the American, Westfall, express technical opinions concerning offshore oil exploration?'

A lot about the Bulgarians. Did Westfall venture personal interest in Bulgarian claims to Yugoslav Macedonia? What statements did Miss Kaladzhiev make regarding the subordinates of her father, the Bulgarian ambassador? Did Miss Kaladzhiev express sympathy for or contact with members of the Bulgarian dissident movement?

And so on. Day after day. As befit their training and indoctrination nobody showed much emotion, but I could sense that higher up in the organisation there was panic that the Americans had penetrated our planning and communications systems. At times interest in my own activity seemed secondary compared to preoccupation with the security slip-up of our Bulgarian confederates.

It was a Thursday, I believe, late in the afternoon when I was summoned to the limousine and driven into central Moscow. By now I had grown accustomed to my routine and this change in the daily interrogation pattern stirred my entrails with anxiety. Was I to be transferred to a prison? Were court proceedings to commence?

The driver swerved down the long avenues and turned into the courtyard of an official building in the street Morisa Toreza, 26. I was escorted to an empty conference room where I was kept waiting alone for ten minutes. Then I heard my name called. I stepped through an adjoining door to a large office.

'Good afternoon, Papa,' I said to Ing. Sokolovskiy.

'Take a chair,' said the Soviet Minister of Petroleum and Mining from behind his large oak desk. Olga's father wore a conservative, double-breasted grey suit. His thick neck strained against his shirt collar as he rumpled his hand through his flowing white, orchestra leader's hair. He watched me balefully before he opened a cabinet shelf and set two glasses and an unlabelled litre bottle on the desk blotter in front of him.

'You'll drink vodka?' he grumbled.

I stepped over and poured a quarter-litre portion which I swallowed rapidly, then poured another glass in quick succession. That place where I was being detained was run like a temperance society for all its conveniences.

'Aye, drink it down. It's the best of illegal home brew,' he watched me with cold eyes. 'A gift of affection from my personal chauffeur. And far too grand for you, you son of a bitch.'

'I would only . . .'

'You *would* what? Don't speak your fancified Russian to me!' he roared. 'I consider you a degenerate, a parasite! You have defiled your career service, burrowed into positions of importance, wormed your way into a state of trust and confidence. Your government you betray, your wife you reject, all to revel in the sweaty pleasures of a Bulgarian whore!'

Red spots glowed at his temples as his voice rose in fury. He kicked back his chair, rattled the glasses on his desk with rage, strode to the window and turned his back on me.

'Had I been that ambassador of yours in Vienna I would have had you gelded!' The windowpane rattled from his shout. 'Spayed you, cut you like a eunuch! Then we would need no dispositions. There would be no tonnage of documentation on your indiscretions. No giggling behind my back in the corridors of this my ministry that my son-in-law has turned pimp and procurer!'

Since my return to Moscow I had been a model of apathy, but now I was angered.

'Stop your lecture. Summon your fancy driver and tell my keepers to throw me into the Lubyanka. Everything you say has a basis in fact. But I will not be abused and denigrated.'

He clamped his teeth and glared at me in fury. The taut cords of his neck strained like wire cables of a construction derrick. He smacked his fist against the window frame, paced back to the desk and poured two glasses of vodka. He motioned to my glass and popped the cork back in the bottle.

'Very well,' he said quietly straining to control his emotion.

'*Na zdorovye.*'

'*Na zdorovye*,' I replied, touching his glass with a clink.

Hurling his bulk into his chair he dug his elbows into the desk blotter and stared at me.

'Now you listen, get it straight, because it has taken a damn great effort of research to find out what they are going to do to you. Ready?'

'I ask nothing of you,' I replied evenly. 'I bear full responsibility for my own actions.'

'Bravo, most noble, but you listen to me and forget the heroics. Tomorrow morning you will be summoned to a formal sitting of your organisation's judicial section. This is not a trial. It is not a public court. It is an administrative tribunal. To pronounce judgement and – or – sentence. The dispositions you have been making over the past weeks have been compared with the testimony of other KGB officials.'

'What officials?'

'I am unable to confirm the entire list. But you will be faced tomorrow by your erstwhile *Rezident*, Chervenkov, and your Vienna embassy security chief, one Razin.'

'Then it's all stacked. The tribunal will exonerate those two and pack me off to the labour camp.'

'Youth knows all,' Papa stared to heaven with soulful eyes and fought for patience. 'Are you going to listen? All three of you are under inquisition. Chervenkov, because a *Rezident* is responsible for all the misdemeanours of his underlings. Razin, because a security chief is supposed to run a tight ship and is in trouble if the crew starts to mutiny. And Sergei, young, bright, cosmopolitan Sergei, is in much trouble for slight lapses we need not here recapitulate.'

'With Razin's story on record I won't have a prayer. God alone knows what he has told them.'

'God alone cannot, however, swap his weekend cottage with one of the tribunal commissioners. Nor offer employment in the Petroleum Ministry to the nephew of another. There are five bastard commissioners on that panel . . .

'And you have squared two of them.'

'Don't be shocked, son, it's done every day. Pity that I couldn't get to the other three. But, maybe they will simply judge your case by the old-fashioned criteria of truth and merit.'

'And if those three vote against me?' I questioned, my voice choked with helplessness.

He hunched his thick shoulders.

'What can I say in consolation? I am told, ten years' sentence at minimum. But don't think I sympathise from mere charity. I am fighting for my own skin. If you go, I go. Your sentence will bring my enemies howling down upon me. I wouldn't last another week in this Ministry and would be expelled from the Central Committee with disgrace and abuse.'

'You know why the Americans did this to us?' I said gloomily. 'You have been told that they staged this entire operation? As a threat to force future Soviet petroleum concessions?'

He grunted, lifting the palms of his powerful hands.

'I do not need to pound my chest and bellow that I will not be cowed. Eh, but these American bastards make their point.'

'Do not concede them one drop of petroleum!'

'Don't be alarmed, my dear fellow patriot. But, I must say, should there arise a situation in the future when Americans have bid against other Western competitors, and all other conditions being equal . . .'

'You'll give them a deal,' I said quietly, knowing that in his own way Westfall had won.

'They'll get the deal. In that circumstance. After all,' he snorted, 'we must continue to exist on the same planet with these cowboys.'

Dear God, I could not stand ten years in penal incarceration. The privations, the humiliation, I perhaps could face with some kind of stoicism. But I could not exist without Olga and our son Anatoli for the next ten years of my life. Not now, not at this one moment when I had finally begun to comprehend the worth, the value, which Olga now signified for me.

'I want to see Olga and Anatoli. My jailers have prevented me from reaching my own wife and son.'

'And what have we here?' Papa roared, smacking his glass on the table. 'A gallows recantation? A deathbed conversion? You are still stinking with the perfumes of that Bulgarian bitch and now show remorse for your family and contrition for your sins of neglect?'

I watched him tiredly.

'When may I at least see them?'

'That depends on your hearing tomorrow,' he knotted his hands together and watched me with grey eyes. 'Olga will be allowed to wait outside the tribunal chambers. Either she will see you for five minutes before you are led away to serve sentence in a distant place. Or . . .'

'Tell me!'

'Or, you walk away with her a free man,' he shrugged. 'I wouldn't bet on it except for one element.'

I looked into his eyes, struggling for hope.

'You see,' Dipl. Ing. G. V. Sokolovskiy stated, 'you came home.'

They arrived for me at nine the next morning. There were two of them, one was a driver and the second was a thick-shouldered enforcer with the job of preventing me from straying off to the Bolshoi Ballet or nipping into the Pushkin Museum while en route to my tribunal. The windshield wipers slapped against the oily drizzle as we drove through the city suburbs, turned along the embankment of the Moscow river, and bumped through the puddles in the broken asphalt before we drove down the ramp of a large concrete administrative building. This was another of the anonymous structures which represent such a high proportion of KGB real-estate holdings. I shivered in the dampness of the ill-ventilated underground garage. My warders put me into an elevator, pressed the automatic control button for the fifth floor, strode down the maze of dimly lit corridors, as if this wasn't the first time they had followed this routine, and escorted me into the anteroom of the tribunal chambers.

I stood there in a white synthetic shirt which was open at the collar and realised that my costume was the first sign that the tribunal was biassed against me. Had I retained a scrap of favour, I rationalised, someone would have provided a cravat to enhance my bruised dignity. Necktie-less, I was only one degree removed from shaven head and prison denim.

Precisely on the stroke of 10:00am the door swung open and the muscular escort nodded for me to enter. I walked into the tribunal chamber.

Facing me was a long veneer table. Seated in the centre were the five commissioners. Each end of the table was occupied by a KGB stenographer.

Three individual tables and straight-back chairs were placed opposite the tribunal. At the table on the far right sat the thick, burly Chervenkov, my *Rezident* from Vienna, his black hair brushed back over his crown like ram's horns. He wore a dark business suit, white starched shirt and grey necktie, signs that he remained much in favour.

Slouched behind the table at the far left of the room was Vienna embassy security chief, Razin. Coatless, with necktie. Down one notch in the sartorial stakes, but still keeping his foot in. I noticed that the capillaries of his scalp were inflamed and disfigured. His eyes were full of bilious film.

I was motioned to occupy the centre table where I sat directly opposite the tribunal commissioners, faceless bureaucrats in shiny blue suits. The chamber's walls were whitewashed a dirty shade of grey. Through the narrow windows I could see rain falling. The wall above the tribunal was graced with an oil portrait of V. I. Lenin; a photograph of our current president of the Union of Soviet Socialist Republics; and a grainy photo of the chairman of the Committee for State Security. None of them looked particularly joyous.

The hefty bloke, the thick-shouldered type who had led me to the chamber, took seat directly behind me with his back to a door leading away from the chamber. No pug-faced militia appeared with bayonets and automatic rifles, but I supposed they were available with reasonable alacrity were they to be paged.

One of the commissioners rapped an American-type ball-point pen against his water glass and signalled that the proceedings were to begin. There were many references to paragraphs such and such of regulations so and so. Citation was made of dispositions taken in Moscow, photocopies of telegraphic prints from the Vienna embassy were referred to, and standing procedures were cited which made it clear that the purpose of the tribunal was to pronounce findings already reached *in camera*. That meant that the five commissioners, two of whom were allegedly squared by my father-in-law, knew what they were pronouncing on me, but I didn't know. Chervenkov and Razin didn't know either, and that was why Chervenkov kept slicking back his hair and two spots of perspiration began to spread under Razin's armpits. As he sweated the sticky scent of his perfume lilted over to my nostrils.

'. . . charges are summarised, following: . . .' the pale presiding commissioner was reading from a prepared document. The stenographers scribbled on their note pads. '. . . One. Said defendant . . .' he meant me, '. . . did wilfully assist the defection of a national from allied Socialist power. Two. Did initiate unlawful embezzlement of embassy finances . . .' the pale official read three more clauses, but those were superfluous since I could draw ten years as an incarcerated guest of the Soviet state on the first two counts.

Then they spoke their case against Chervenkov. He was allegedly involved in oversight and failure to supervise my adherence to procedures. It was pretty tame and watery.

Then came remarks about Razin. I heard such verbage as 'delinquent', and 'obsession with vendetta', plus a few 'failures to exercise discipline of embassy technical personnel'. He was squirming in his chair and I wasn't but my forehead burned with a hot band of worry.

'Comrade Chervenkov.'

The presiding commissioner nodded curtly to my *Rezident* who rose and advanced to stand in front of the tribunal.

'While administrative shortcomings of your Vienna tenure will be noted in your personal file, you are exonerated from further inquiry. Transfer at this time from your post would be detrimental to the interests of this service. You are to return immediately to the

Vienna embassy.'

Chervenkov accepted this reprieve in glacial silence. He swung around and strode past me and passed through the large doors at the rear of the chamber.

'Comrade Razin?'

Razin fumbled at his necktie knot, skidded his chair back, and advanced to face the commissioners.

'Comrade Razin, as chief of Vienna embassy security you have evidenced failure to grasp the full import of your administrative responsibilities,' the blank faced presiding officer read from a typed document. 'You have adopted negativist and defensive attitudes. Furthermore . . .'

'Not one penetration!' Razin yelped. 'Not one document has left my embassy! No member of the embassy staff . . .'

The commissioner rapped once with the ball-point pen against the water glass. Razin gestured helplessly with upturned hands only to wilt in silence as the commissioner continued with his recitation.

'Furthermore, your suitability for an assignment outside the confines of the Soviet Union appears misfounded. This was witnessed by the crude, illegal, inappropriate attempt to employ means of violence on foreign territory.' Razin was being chastised for his potshots at me across rainy Austrian fields.

'Our finding,' the commissioner concluded, 'is that Comrade Razin will not return to his Vienna post. He is reassigned as officer of internal security, Red October Machine Tools Plant no. 2, District of Volgograd. Further foreign assignments cancelled.'

Razin uttered a guttural croak and stood back cowed by the icy stares of the tribunal. He turned and glared at me with venom. He flung his hands upward, faltered at his table, then slouched out of the room and out of my life.

The pen rang once again against the water glass. My turn.

I rose from the table, strode forward to face the panel, and stood there rigid and erect, inwardly resigned to the whip-lash sentence that would now flail across my shoulders.

'This tribunal first wishes to record its revulsion at the lack of moral discretion evidenced by the defendant . . .' My eyes had turned hazy and I could see nothing beyond the featureless image of the presiding officer in his department-store blue suit. His censure pounded in my ears, my character was stretched in pathological autopsy, my weaknesses were dissected and pinned for documentation in microscopic detail. All this I could, however, accept. I could deal with the personal humiliation, the shame, the wreckage of my ambitions. But fear for Sokolovskiy gnawed at my soul. Once I was sentenced his enemies would utilise my failings to wreck his career. He would be driven into the cold, hounded by his opponents and abandoned by his friends. And my conviction by this tribunal would deprive my son Anatoli of his father, his father who had in sensual selfishness abdicated any sense of love or concern. But beyond all considerations my disgrace would deprive me of Olga. I would be sentenced and led into the corridors and would see her standing at a distance, only to be dragged from her life for the next ten years. Could she wait for me? Why should I inflict that final humiliation upon her? I would instruct her to seek a divorce and rid herself of this man who had brought her nothing but punishment and disgrace . . .

I stood there ramrod straight and felt tears of remorse blotting my sight. Prisms of light danced across my vision. The room tilted at an angle, the five commissioners slid down the table and merged into the presiding official who droned a catalogue of my delinquencies, then they separated and wiggled back to the ends of the table.

'*Izvinitye*?' I mumbled incoherently. They had asked me a question which I had not understood.

'Do you hereby acknowledge . . .' the flat-toned commissioner repeated his question, 'that you have responded to the dispositions of this tribunal without pressure or duress?'

I nodded dumbly, not grasping the question.

'As chairman of this tribunal,' the official continued, 'I ask my colleagues for their voice on the principal decision of disciplinary measures. Approving?' he queried the other four commissioners. He was looking for the positive vote that would send me off to the prisons for the next decade.

By some geometric accident the two commissioners on each end of the table raised their fists in a *za* vote approving condemnation.

The stenographers scribbled their names into the record.

'And for exoneration?' demanded the presiding commissioner.

Hesitatingly, the official on the left of the presiding officer raised his index finger. That was it. Two to one and the others need not make a poll of it.

Then, very slowly, the official on the other flank of the chairman raised his arm in a vote of acquittal.

I stared at them blankly. Two-two.

'In view of this deadlock, my duties require me to take a decision,' droned the presiding commissioner.

It was all going by a pre-arranged script. The two officials who had been bought by Ing. Sokolovskiy had thrown their lots in my direction, but now this final blank-faced bastard was going to vote *za* for condemnation, rob Sergei of his freedom and take me away from my family.

'Comrade . . .' he addressed me by my patronymic, '. . . if I may inject a personal note, I wish to state my thorough disgust for your failures of character.' He was also a sadist, who obviously enjoyed the pleasure of dangling me on the hooks. State your sentence! I nearly screamed . . .

'But we in this service also place value on courage. Particularly when faced by misguided, homicidal attempts intended to prevent your return to the Soviet Union. My vote is, thus, *protiv*.'

It was three-two against prosecution.

I had no choice other than to lean my rump against the table for support. It wasn't particularly dignified, but the ligaments of my knees retained the strength of a glass of yogurt. Clashing cymbals of oxygen pounded through my brain. I fought against an uncontrolled sobbing from my chest.

'. . . shall be ineligible for foreign assignment until case reviewed,' the chairman was pronouncing upon me. One month ago that restriction would have wracked me like chains and fetters but now it seemed completely irrelevant. '. . . to be reassigned to economic assessment branch, NATO area, with specific assignments economic policies of US and United Kingdom . . .' I was being placed in an analytical slot in the KGB Moscow economic branch. Papa Sokolovskiy's work. He had tipped the vote and then convinced them to assign me to a job with some shred of future advancement.

'My signature?' I questioned hazily.

'Sign the documents,' the commissioner stated with obvious disgust.

Gingerly he handed me his ball-point pen and I signed my name across the final lot of dispositions, charges and exonerations.

I looked up at the five of them.

The chairman snapped his fingers. The chamber doors were thrown open. I turned my back to the commissioners and walked out of the chamber and turned down the corridor.

Olga had stood up from a hard wooden bench and was running up the long corridor. I burst towards her, opened my arms and drew her to my chest. Her blonde hair was longer and was brushed straight and sleek across her shoulders. Quietly I stroked her head as she nuzzled against my shoulder.

'I allowed my hair to grow,' she said quietly, looking at me with those grey-flecked eyes. Her skin was exceptionally fair but her cheeks glowed as with warmth of reflected fire. 'It was to be a surprise. And a celebration. The thesis was accepted. They gave me my doctorate, Sergei.'

We stood in the dreary corridor of a faceless building owned by the Soviet Committee for State Security and I felt the pressure of her breasts against me, the warmth of her tall body flowing to my iced chill veins, the pulse of desire and affection which I had by any sane judgement totally forfeited.

'The professors objected to one mathematical model . . .' She had fixed my vision with her distant grey eyes.

'If it is possible,' I stated haltingly, 'I wish, formally, to request . . .'

'. . . then they realised I had used a model developed by one of the members of the examination board.' She watched me, unsmiling.

'I wish formally to request your forgiveness,' I halted, unable to deal with the vectors of conflict slicing my emotions. Freedom. Remorse. The love of a man for his wife. Physical desire to caress my wife. Shame. Exhaustion. Hope. 'I would request . . .'

'No, no, Sergei, no,' and she kissed me, kissed me sensually, drew me to her body, kissed me with licence as we clung to each other alone in a twilight corridor on a rainy Moscow afternoon.

'You need never ask forgiveness,' she stated softly, tossing her ash-blonde hair and watching me with chill concentration. 'But neither will I ask you to absolve my emotional decisions. What I did with my own life, my doctorate, the award and recognition I sought and received, I did with conscious knowledge.'

'I betrayed you.'

'You behaved. You behaved in reaction to my decisions, and, additionally, you followed your own fantasy and impulses. Your behaviour was unfortunate and perhaps childish, but it was not betrayal.'

'I am behaving now by saying that my existence is void if I must live it alone without you and our son.'

'Then it is uncomplicated,' she smiled, her pale cheeks, the peaches-and-cream cheeks of heroines in university novels read so long ago, flushing with warmth. 'It is simple. We continue. We continue with everything that is peaceful and normal and sane. Anatoli has ice-hockey training. He knows that, perhaps, you may join the other fathers watching their sons. He has been at many practices with no father.'

My stomach cramped as I turned to face the grim rain. There would have been many more fatherless practices had not Papa Sokolovskiy swung the tribunal decision.

'Our financial future is not particularly brilliant,' I

said, staring at the foggy afternoon. 'Whatever my salary is going to be, it's not going to be the equivalent of my Vienna payments. Forget the free apartment, the automobiles and dazzling life of the young diplomat.'

She took my arm and turned me back from the window to face her.

'Papa told me the details. Why, and how, you are here. That you would not surrender. That you were injured. Had they aimed slightly higher, my husband,' she smiled, 'had they raised the telescopic sight an additional centimetre, then we would not be holding one another talking about the lack of automobiles.'

I clasped her to me, pressed her to my chest, kissed the cool Arctic blonde hair and watched the grey eyes that spoke of different horizons from figs and olives and hot stones under Balkan suns, and took my wife's arm and walked with her from the tribunal chambers. We stood in the rain by the autobus queue and the bus splashed through the water which had collected in the depressions in the asphalt and I boarded the bus with my wife Olga and we drove to see our son at his hockey training.